The FEATHER MERCHANTS

& Other Tales of the Fools of Chelm

A Richard Jackson Book

Also by Steve Sanfield
The Adventures of High John the Conqueror
A Natural Man: The True Story of John Henry

The FEATHER MERCHANTS
& Other Tales of the Fools of Chelm

by STEVE SANFIELD

illustrated by MIKHAIL MAGARIL

ORCHARD BOOKS   *New York*

Orchard Books
387 Park Avenue South, New York, NY 10016

Manufactured in the United States of America
Book design by Mina Greenstein
The text of this book is set in 12 point Baskerville.
The illustrations are pen-and-ink drawings.
10   9   8   7   6   5   4   3   2   1

Library of Congress Cataloging-in-Publication Data
Sanfield, Steve.
The feather merchants, and other tales of the fools of Chelm /
 by Steve Sanfield ; illustrated by Mikhail Magaril.   p.   cm.
"A Richard Jackson book"—Half title p.
Includes bibliographical references. Summary: Thirteen
traditional Eastern European Jewish tales of the town of Chelm
and its silly citizens.
ISBN 0-531-05958-8.   ISBN 0-531-08558-9 (lib. bdg.)
1. Legends, Jewish. [1. Folklore, Jewish. 2. Chelm (Chelm,
Poland)—Folklore.]   I. Magaril, Mikhail, ill.   II. Title.
III. Title: Feather merchants.
PZ8.1.S242Fe   1991   398.2—dc20   [E]   90-29273

FOR MY GRANDFATHERS

Mikhail Bernstein
1877–1959

Chaim Shanfeld
1865–1937

Labish Weintrab
1884–1967

May their memory be a blessing.

Contents

Foreword, 1

A Beginning, 2
The Shul, 8
The Rabbi, 12
Oyzar the Scholar, 18
The Mikva, 30
Pinkhes the Peddler, 38
Yossel and Sossel, 44
Berish the Shammes, 50
A Celebration, 56
The Inn of the Stolen Moon, 60
Elders and Riddlers, 70
The Feather Merchants, 76
The Council of Seven Sages, 84

Afterword, 91
Glossary, 98
Bibliography, 101

אַ צעבראָכענער זייגער איז בעסער
ווי איינער וואָס גייט ניט ריכטיק:
אויף יעדן פֿאַל איז עס כאָטש ריכטיק צוויי מאָל אין טאָג.

A broken clock is still better
than one that goes wrong:
At least it's right twice a day.

Foreword

ENJOY!
We'll talk later.

A Beginning

The Founding Fathers of Chelm
looked out across the broad,
flat valley below.

A wide river sparkled in the sunshine
as it meandered slowly from east to west.

Like an immense pair of arms hugging a child in a snug embrace, soft, rolling hills encircled the valley on three sides.

Here and there chestnuts and maples mingled with birches and beeches, creating a dozen shades of dancing greenery.

And where the men stood, near the top of the mountain to the north, grew the towering pines and firs with which they planned to build their town.

After the proper prayers and ceremonies of dedication, they began their great work. They selected the largest and strongest trees. Nothing less would do. They carefully felled and limbed the sturdiest ones, but immediately a problem arose.

How were they to get these huge logs down to the valley?

The early Chelmites had no beasts of burden, no carts or wagons. All those would come later. But it is said, "When you must, you can," so the men simply lifted the logs onto their shoulders, a dozen to each, and, amid much huffing and puffing, they carried them down the mountain.

While all this activity was going on, a stranger happened to be passing through the valley. He watched in amazement as the men of Chelm struggled and wrestled with their heavy burdens.

"This is ridiculous," he said to himself. "These men are fools," which may have been the first time anyone ever applied that term to the good people of Chelm.

The stranger joined the workers up on the mountain and suggested they try another way. He gave one of the logs a hearty kick, and it rolled down into the valley as if it knew exactly where it was going.

"Remarkable! A genius!" exclaimed the Chelmites. They immediately descended into the valley, hoisted the logs on their shoulders once more, and, with muscles straining and eyes popping, carried them back up the mountain. Then, one by one, they *rolled* their logs back down.

CHELM, as you probably already suspect, is a very special place, a place where remarkable things are always happening. It is a place where tears and laughter live close together, a place where kindness and sweetness and silliness fill the air.

Chelm is special because its people are special. They are like no others, for, you see, each and every Chelmite, regardless of position or vocation, is a Sage. They are all wise men and women. At least that's what they tell themselves.

That the rest of the world considers them to be fools and simpletons does not bother them in the least. They know they are the wisest people on earth, and in the end, isn't that all that matters?

How, you may ask, did all these fools, or Sages, as the Chelmites prefer to call themselves, end up in one place?

A good question, but as is often the case when dealing

with profound mysteries, there are many different explanations, none of which agree with one another. However, of the infinite number of possibilities, two stand out.

THE FIRST reminds us that the *Torah* says, "God watches over the simple." Now, in his boundless wisdom, knowing there is no way to predict what a simpleton may do, God gathered them all in one place so that it would be easier to keep an eye on them.

The second explanation, which is widely accepted by those who have given the matter serious consideration, is an old legend that tells us that, after God had created the world and everything upon it, there still remained two groups of souls to be distributed—those of the very, very wise and those of the very, very foolish.

It would be only fair to distribute such unique souls equally. Everywhere there were to be a few of the very wise and a few of the very foolish. This way every community would have those who might create problems and those who might solve them, even though one person's solution might well be another person's problem.

God prepared two separate sacks containing the souls of each. Then he instructed an angel to fly over the earth and leave a few from each sack here, a few from each sack there.

However, as the angel was flying over the high mountains just north of Chelm, he flew too close to the jagged peaks. The sack containing the foolish souls caught on a sharp outcrop and tore open. Down they poured into the valley below, where they have lived ever since.

The Shul

The most important single building in any Jewish town is the *shul*, or synagogue. It serves, not only as the House of Prayer and the House of Study, but also as a communal meeting place, so naturally it was the first structure to be built in Chelm.

The first men of Chelm started digging the *shul*'s foundation, but a disturbing thought occurred to one of them.

"What," he asked, "are we going to do with all this dirt we're digging up? We can't just leave it here where we're going to have our *shul*."

"We never thought of that," declared the others. "What, indeed, are we going to do with all this dirt?"

Many suggestions were made, but all were quickly rejected as unworkable.

"I have it!" shouted the same man who had posed the question in the first place. "All we have to do is dig a deep pit, and into it we'll shovel the dirt we're digging up for the foundation."

This suggestion was received with cheers, and the men began to dig another pit. They'd hardly broken the surface of the earth when someone else called out, "Wait a minute. This doesn't solve anything. What are we going to do with the dirt from this hole?"

The digging stopped as quickly as it had begun. Shovels hung in midair, for suddenly here was an entirely new problem: what to do with the dirt from the second hole?

It seemed like an impossible situation, but as would become the tradition in Chelm, an ordinary townsman saved the day. "It's really very simple," he said. "We'll just dig one more pit twice as large as this one, and into that we'll shovel all the dirt from this hole *and* all the dirt from the foundation."

There was no arguing with this early example of Chelmic logic, and the men returned to their work.

THE BUILDING of the synagogue took the entire summer

and a good part of the fall, but it was ready in time to celebrate *Rosh Hashanah*, the Jewish New Year. And what a grand celebration it was—a new synagogue, a new town, a new beginning.

As soon as the Days of Awe were over, everyone devoted all their energies to helping their neighbors finish their new homes. Doors were hung, roofs were covered, and by the time the first icy winds blew through the streets of Chelm, everyone was comfortably settled in their humble dwelling.

But that first winter was a difficult one, a very difficult one.

It arrived early and stayed late. Snow covered the ground for weeks at a time, often rising high enough to meet the icicles that hung down from the roofs. Cold chilled the bones until no one could even remember what it was like to be warm.

The little firewood that had been cut was soon gone. All that remained in the stoves and fireplaces were ashes, and ashes have never been known to keep anybody or anything warm. Shaking and shivering, people took to burning their own furniture, so that by the time the healing warmth of spring finally reached the valley, everyone was sitting on the floor.

It had been a terrible time. It was a miracle they all survived.

A town meeting was called. The prospect of another freezing winter was discussed, deliberated, and dissected. There was no dispute and no debate: everyone agreed that such discomfort should never be allowed to happen again. The solution? As simple as *aleph-beys*. The Chelmites built a high brick wall around the town to keep out the cold.

The Rabbi

Among the wisest of all Chelmites was the rabbi (would you expect anything less?), so wise, in fact, he often came up with answers to dilemmas that had nothing to do with the life of the spirit.

An example: a terrible occurrence. A thief had stolen the poor box from the synagogue. (Yes, Chelm had its thieves, just like every other town.) Who'd ever heard of such a thing—stealing money meant for the very poorest among the people?

What was to be done? Put up another poor box? The thief, if he'd been that desperate in the first place, would only steal it again. Not put one up? What kind of synagogue would it be without a poor box?

This was a serious problem indeed, but no problem was ever too difficult for the deep wisdom of the Chelmites, especially when many minds worked together. The directors of the synagogue held a meeting to examine the situation. They discussed, deliberated, and dissected, and it wasn't long before they arrived at a solution. A new poor box would be hung close to the ceiling, so high up that no thief, unless he could fly, would ever be able to reach it.

As the directors were congratulating themselves on their own sagaciousness, Berish the *Shammes*, who was responsible for the upkeep of the synagogue, pointed out that although no thief would be able to get at the poor box, neither would anyone else, thus making it impossible to leave a donation.

Here was an even more serious problem, since giving to charity was a joy and an honor as well as a duty.

Finally the rabbi stepped in and resolved the quandary. A ladder would be built to allow the charitable to reach the poor box and leave their donations. And to prevent thieves from using it, a sign would be hung declaring,

> ONLY FOR THOSE WISHING TO MAKE DONATIONS
> NO THIEVES ALLOWED

Is it any wonder, then, that the people of Chelm put faith in their rabbi when it came to matters secular as well as spiritual? He was like the sages of old, always ready to help no matter how complicated the situation.

Baruch the Bookbinder once came to him and said, "Rabbi, my son, Yossel, is about to have his *Bar Mitzvah*. He has studied *Torah* and *Talmud*, the history of our people, the responsibilities that come with being thirteen. All this he knows well. He's about to reach his manhood, and I think I should tell him something about the birds and the bees, but I don't know what to say."

"First of all," the eminent rabbi replied, "forget about the birds and the bees."

"Forget about the birds and the bees? Why?"

"Because it's just not so."

"It's not so? But, Rabbi, how can you say that?"

"I can say it because it's true, and I know it's true because I proved it. You see, I too had always heard about the birds and the bees, but I wanted to see with my own eyes. I captured a bird and I captured a bee. Then I put them in a cage together for three days and three nights. I watched them constantly, and I tell you that nothing, absolutely nothing happened."

YOSSEL BECAME *Bar Mitzvah*, and a few years later it was time for him to marry. In those days in Chelm, as elsewhere, it was still the custom to prearrange marriages. Parents would often make such decisions while their children were still very young, and sometimes the bride-and-groom-to-be did not actually meet until shortly before the wedding.

Such was the case here. Yossel was about to meet his

future wife, Sossel, for the first time, and, being not particularly experienced in the ways of the world, he went to the rabbi to ask for some advice.

"Rabbi, I'm going to visit my Sossel tomorrow, but I have no idea of what to say to her. Can you help me?"

The rabbi smiled warmly and said, "It's simple, my boy. Men and women have been getting married since Adam and Eve, and very little has changed. When you see your fiancée, first talk to her about love. Then speak about family. And finally, finish up with a little philosophy. That should take care of everything."

Yossel thanked the rabbi and went on his way, all the time repeating the rabbi's advice, "Love, family, philosophy. Love, family, philosophy."

The next day, when he arrived at his intended's house, her parents were there to greet him. He couldn't very well speak of such intimate things in front of them, but as soon as the young couple was left alone, Yossel blurted out, "Tell me. Do you love noodles?"

"Yes, I love noodles," she answered, a little surprised. "Why shouldn't I love noodles?"

Yossel had no idea how to answer her question, so he said nothing. There was a long silence, and then he asked, "Tell me, do you have a brother?"

"No, I don't have a brother," she replied.

Ah, thought Yossel, *this is going to be easier than I thought. I've already taken care of love and family. Now, just as the rabbi told me, all I have to do is finish with a little philosophy.*

There was an even longer silence as Yossel strained for the right words. Finally he said, "Tell me, if you had a brother, would he love noodles?"

[16]

THE RABBI'S ADVICE seemed to work, because Yossel did marry Sossel. But it wasn't long before he was back at the rabbi's, this time excited and clearly upset.

"Rabbi," he pleaded, close to tears, "you've got to help me. My wife just had a baby."

"Why, *mazel tov*," said the rabbi. "Congratulations. Children are the greatest joy of all. The pleasures they bring are more precious than gold. Besides, you're fulfilling the commandment: 'Be fruitful and multiply.' Why should you need my help?"

"You don't understand, Rabbi. We've been married only three months, and my mother told me herself that it takes a baby nine months to be born."

"My son," said the rabbi kindly, "your mother spoke the truth, but there is no problem that cannot be solved with the help of the proper logic properly applied. Now let me ask you a few questions. Have you lived with your wife for three months?"

"Yes, Rabbi."

"Has she lived with you for three months?"

"Yes, Rabbi."

"And you've lived together for three months?"

"Yes, Rabbi."

"Well, then. What's the total of three months plus three months plus three months?"

"Nine months, Rabbi."

"There!" the rabbi said. "Nine months, just as your mother told you. Now go home to your wife and child and rejoice."

Oyzar the Scholar

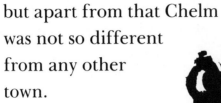

It is true that Chelm, from the first, was filled with Sages, and it's also true that remarkable things were always happening to them, but apart from that Chelm was not so different from any other town.

Chelmites were merchants and beggars, butchers and bakers, tailors and cobblers. They were drivers and drovers, woodcutters and water carriers, teachers and scholars.

Actually, because everyone was so wise to begin with, there were more scholars in Chelm than a pine tree has needles. However, among them was one who stood above the rest, one who was known to everyone as The Scholar. His name was Oyzar—Oyzar the Scholar, to be precise.

Oyzar was well aware that in past generations the most respected members of the community, whether it be large or small, were the scholars. Who has not heard that "Learning is the best merchandise"? Yet it was neither riches nor respect that Oyzar desired. He simply loved analyzing and philosophizing—"dreaming," his wife called it. He spent his days and nights studying and thinking. He liked nothing better than to consider difficult and obscure problems that no one else had the time or inclination to approach.

For example, you already know that if you put sugar in a glass of tea (you probably use a cup, but in Chelm tea was always drunk from a glass) and then stir it until it dissolves, the tea, which is bitter to begin with, becomes sweet. This happens to be a fact of nature. It cannot be denied.

But have you ever asked yourself what is it that makes the tea sweet? Is it the sugar, or is it the stirring of the spoon? Before you answer too quickly and embarrass yourself, give some thought to the conclusion that Oyzar reached only after months of study and experimentation.

It is the stirring of the spoon.

Why add the sugar, then, you probably ask. A good question and one that many people have asked Oyzar. After all, if it's the spoon that's responsible for sweetening the tea, why waste the sugar by dissolving it? Well, according to Oyzar's calculations, you add the sugar so you'll know how long to stir the tea. Only when it's completely dissolved can you be sure the tea is sweet enough to drink.

ONCE, early in the springtime, just after the feast of *Purim*, Oyzar was busy trying to make sense of a curious question a young man named Shmuel had brought to him that very morning. Shmuel, although still a student (his secret ambition was to become a scholar and philosopher like Oyzar), was well past the age when he should have had a respectable beard, but no hairs grew on his chin, not a single one. He had a fine head of curly hair but no beard. His chin was as smooth as a newborn baby's.

"What could it be?" he asked Oyzar. "I'm strong and healthy. I eat well. I get plenty of rest, but no hair grows on my face like the other young men's. How can I become a true Sage like you if I don't have a beard like you?"

"True, all too true," said Oyzar, stroking his own bushy, gray beard. "Unless, of course, it's hereditary."

"No," said Shmuel, "that's impossible. My father and his father before him each had long, full beards that covered up half their bellies."

"Well, there must be a logical explanation," suggested Oyzar. "There always is. Why don't you let me think about it for a while? Come back this evening. Perhaps I'll have an answer for you."

Beardless Shmuel left Oyzar alone to ponder. The Scholar searched his books, but nowhere could he find a single clue to explain Shmuel's naked face.

Morning became afternoon, and as the day grew

warmer Oyzar opened the window to cool his study and his
mind. A soft breeze entered. It carried with it the sweet scent
of the first crocuses and the cleansing air of the season. It
also carried the laughing voices of children playing under
the window.

Oyzar was fond of children, and they of him. He spent much of his time with them, playing games and teasing them with riddles. On any other day he might well have joined them outside, but today their play was disturbing his concentration. He didn't want to hurt their feelings by telling them they weren't welcome around his house. Still, he had promised Shmuel an answer.

"Children," he called, leaning out the window. "Do you know what today is? Today is the day the great dragon of the sea is supposed to swim up our river."

The children stopped their romping. "Dragon? What dragon?" they asked, for as far as they knew no dragon had ever been seen in Chelm.

"The dragon of the sea," Oyzar explained. "He's twenty feet long, with the head of a lion and the body of a gigantic fish. He has the wings of an eagle and the horns of a bull. He swims in the water and breathes fire and smoke. He travels all over the world, visiting every river once every hundred and twenty years, and today is the day he's supposed to come to ours. If you see him you will have good luck forever, but you'd better go quickly or the dragon will have already swum past Chelm."

The children needed no further encouragement. Off they ran to the river, laughing all the way, and Oyzar settled down determined to find an answer to Shmuel's dilemma.

He had barely begun when he was disturbed by the shouting of a crowd of people rushing after the children. "Where are you all going in such a hurry?" he asked from his window.

"To the river, to the river," someone yelled. "Haven't you heard? There's a fire-breathing dragon there that comes only once in a man's lifetime."

For a moment Oyzar the Scholar was tempted to join the crowd. When else might he have a chance to see such a creature? But then he remembered that he himself had made up the story to get the children to leave him in peace and quiet. He shook his head in wonder over the power of a simple rumor.

He'd barely sat down at his desk again when he heard another commotion in the street below his window. It was the entire Council of Seven Sages and their families hurrying toward the river.

"Where are you all off to?" Oyzar called.

"To the river to see the dragon," replied one of the Sages. "Come quickly. There's a huge dragon who devours lions and eagles but gives his blessing to people."

Oyzar grabbed his coat and ran into the street. *Who*

knows? he thought to himself. *If even the Council of Seven Sages, the wisest of the wise, believes there's a dragon in the river, it's probably so, and I wouldn't want to be the only one to miss it.*

By the time he reached the river, everybody else was on their way back to town. Most were grumbling and shaking their heads because there was no dragon to be seen anywhere. This didn't discourage Oyzar, however. He wasn't called The Scholar for nothing. A true scholar must prove everything for himself. Otherwise there is no way to know for certain whether something is true or not.

But, alas, even for Oyzar there was no dragon.

As he walked slowly home, he speculated about how such a wild rumor could have got started, but since there was no simple explanation forthcoming, Oyzar moved his mind to the pressing matter of Shmuel's beard, or rather the lack of it.

By the time he arrived back in his study, Oyzar had penetrated the mystery. When Shmuel returned later that evening, Oyzar was ready for him.

"It's clear," Oyzar began, "that your lack of a beard is hereditary."

"Hereditary? How could that be?" Shmuel asked, bewildered. "We both know that my father and my grandfathers all had healthy beards just like everybody else."

"That is true," Oyzar said gently, "and most boys take after their fathers, but you, you must take after your mother."

"That's it!" exclaimed Shmuel, delighted with the news. "I must take after my mother, since she has no beard."

And Shmuel went on his way grateful for the expla-

nation and surer than ever that when he grew up he wanted
to be just like The Scholar.

LATER THAT YEAR, near the end of summer when the days
are long and the dust sits heavily upon the roads, Oyzar's
wife, Perl, went to visit her sister on the far side of Chelm.
Knowing her husband to be the dreamer he was, Perl gave
him very specific and, she thought, very clear instructions.

"If the baby begins to wake up, rock the cradle slowly
and she'll go right back to sleep. If the *tsimmes* starts to boil
over, move it to the back of the stove until it cools down a
bit."

"No need to worry," said Oyzar. "If the baby wakes,
rock her. If the *tsimmes* boils, move it."

Confident that her husband understood, Perl went out
the door, but not a minute had passed and she was back.
She'd remembered the jar of black currant preserves she
had made only a few days before. She'd also remembered
Oyzar's sweet tooth, almost as famous in Chelm as his penetrating wisdom. She wanted to serve the preserves on *Rosh
Hashanah* when they wished each other a sweet year. What
she didn't want was Oyzar devouring them all.

"Oyzar, my love," she said gently. "I forgot to tell you.
Be sure not to touch the fruit jar there on the shelf. It's filled
with rat poison."

"If the baby wakes, rock her. If the *tsimmes* boils, move
it. Don't touch the jar—it's poison. It's all simple enough,"
Oyzar reassured her. "Give my best to your sister, and don't
worry about a thing."

Perl left and Oyzar went to his study, planning to think

his way through a situation that had presented itself the night before in a dream. "Suppose," he began, talking to himself, "all the men in Chelm became one gigantic man, bigger even than Goliath, and then suppose . . ." But he couldn't complete his speculation, because what began to run through his mind were Perl's instructions: "If the baby wakes, rock her. If the *tsimmes* boils, move it. Don't touch the jar—it's poison."

This was an impossible situation. The baby was in the bedroom, the *tsimmes* was in the kitchen, and the jar was in the pantry. How could he possibly keep an eye on everything when everything wasn't in the same place? If he were to spend the morning worrying about such things, he'd never be able to do his own work.

A scrunching of the brow and a squinting of the eyes gave Oyzar his resolution. First, he dragged his own rocking chair from his study to the kitchen. Then he moved the cradle in front of the stove and set the fruit jar on the table next to it. Finally—and this is where he revealed his true genius—he tied one end of a rope to the cradle and the other end to his ankle. From his chair he could now watch the *tsimmes*, rock the cradle, and meditate on his original problem all at once, which is exactly what he did.

Suppose all the men in Chelm became one gigantic man and all the trees on the mountain joined together to become one stupendous tree and all the rivers and lakes and streams somehow flowed together to become one limitless lake. . . .

The sweet *tsimmes* simmered slowly on the stove. The baby slept the sleep only the innocent know. And Oyzar slipped deeper and deeper into his own reverie.

Then suppose this gigantic man picked up a massive ax that had been made from all the axes in the world and proceeded to chop down that stupendous tree, which would then fall into that limitless lake—is there anyone who would be able to imagine the size of the splash it would make?

Such was Oyzar's fantasy . . . and when, after an hour or more, that man finished chopping that tree, which fell into the middle of that lake, the resulting splash in Oyzar's mind was as real as the tongue in his mouth.

With a shout he leaped out of his chair. It turned over. The rope attached to his ankle pulled the cradle, knocked it on its side, and dumped the baby onto the floor.

Oyzar rushed to pick up the baby, who was now shrieking and screaming, but he smashed into the cradle, crashed into the stove, and upended the pot of *tsimmes*, which spilled across the top of the stove and immediately commenced to burn.

This was a disaster, a catastrophe greater than the fall of that gigantic tree.

"Oy, oy, oy, oy," Oyzar moaned. "My wife will never forgive me. Who knows what she'll do?"

There was only one thing for Oyzar to do, and he did it.

When Perl returned, she could scarcely believe the scene that awaited her. The baby lay on her stomach on the floor, bawling and blubbering, her eyes red from tears. The cradle was splintered, its pieces scattered about. The rocking chair, which didn't even belong in the kitchen, lay askew on its side. The fruit jar, which also didn't belong there, was tipped on the table without its cap. The entire house was filled with the nose-wrinkling odor of burned carrots and prunes from the spilled *tsimmes*, which had bubbled and hardened on the stove.

And where was her husband, the esteemed scholar?

He was nowhere to be seen amid this chaos.

Perl heard a low moan from the bedroom, and when she looked, there he was lying in bed with the covers pulled up to his chin. His skin was pale, almost gray, and he had a sad, faraway look in his eyes.

"You *schlemiel*! You fool!" Perl screamed. "I leave you alone for a few hours and you destroy everything. You're worthless. You're worse than good-for-nothing. Look at you lying there in bed as if everything were fine. I should strangle you."

"Shh, please," begged Oyzar. "Speak softly. You won't have to strangle me, although God knows I deserve it. I'll be dead soon anyway."

"Dead? What are you babbling about now?"

"Well," Oyzar continued, "when I saw what I had done, although I'm not exactly sure how it happened . . . You see, there was this enormous splash. . . ."

"Splash? What splash, you idiot!"

"It doesn't matter. It's too late now. When I saw what had happened, I knew you'd never forgive me. I couldn't live with that, so I ate all the poison in the fruit jar, and now I'm dying."

There was nothing Perl could say, at least nothing that would do any good—not that day nor for many days after.

Of course, Oyzar didn't die. Eventually Perl forgave him. He was her husband, and she did love him. He was, after all, The Scholar.

The Mikva

The Founding Fathers of Chelm concluded that if their town was going to take its proper place among others of the world, more public buildings were needed. The Chelmites were justifiably proud of their synagogue, but it wasn't quite enough.

After serious consideration, it was decided that a *mikva*, a ritual bathhouse, should come next, so that prior to each Sabbath, holiday, or special occasion, everyone would be able to bathe correctly.

Once again the men climbed the mountains and felled some of the larger trees. This time, however, they needed no one to show them the best way to get the logs down the slope. They simply gave each one a healthy kick, and just as the trees had done years before, these too rolled to the bottom without having to be told where to go.

But once at the bottom, it was not to be so simple, because Dovid the Barrelmaker asked which end should be carried into town first.

"What do you mean, which end? What difference does it make?" one of the men asked.

"What difference does it make?" Dovid responded. "It makes all the difference in the world. Correct me if I am mistaken, but I believe each of these logs has two ends."

Who could argue? Everyone could see with his own eyes that each log did indeed have two ends.

Dovid continued, "It is well known that the one who goes first is the one most honored, and since we have already honored these logs by choosing them above all others to use in our *mikva*, we must now decide which end should be further honored by being carried into town first."

Of course, this observation made perfect sense to everyone, and a discussion began about which end should be so honored. Those who were right-handed naturally thought it should be the right end, and, just as naturally, those who were left-handed thought it should be the left end.

"Right." "Left." "Right." "Left." "Right." "Left."

Because there were just as many left-handed folk in Chelm as right-handed folk, the debate continued through the afternoon. With darkness gathering, they could see that soon they would be unable to see. They could also see that they were no closer to an agreement than when they started.

Hoping a wisdom more penetrating than their own might settle the matter, they took their problem to Oyzar the Scholar.

"If only all problems were as simple as this one"—Oyzar sighed—"how pleasant life would be. All you need to do is cut off the left end of the log. Then you will have only one end, the right end, and that being the only end left, it will be the right end to carry into town first."

"Another brilliant solution by our distinguished scholar," Dovid declared, and the men returned to their homes that night with easy minds. They met early the next day ready to follow Oyzar's advice and continue with the work of building the bathhouse.

Because it had been Dovid who was the first to realize that honor was not for human beings alone, and because as a barrelmaker he had a lifetime of experience with wood, he was given the honor and responsibility of cutting off the left end of the first log.

He took up his saw and began while his comrades watched. Forward and back and forward again the saw flashed in the morning sun. Sawdust flew, and the tangy scent of pine sap filled the air. The saw cut through the wood, and a thin round fell to the ground. The men cheered, but when they looked closely they saw the log still had two ends. Once again they could not deny what their eyes told them.

"Perhaps you haven't cut off enough," suggested one, and Dovid began again. His saw slid back and forth until another round fell from the log.

Another cheer, but still the log had two ends.

It is written that "where men truly wish to go, there their feet will carry them," and Dovid was not to be put off so easily. With fierce determination, he cut round after round until he was too weary even to lift his saw. Another man took over, and he too cut round after round, but no matter how many ends were cut off, two ends still remained—even though they were now separated by less than a foot of wood.

This would never do. Foot-long logs might be well and good to build a dollhouse, but a bathhouse—never. So back they went to Oyzar the Scholar with their new dilemma.

Oyzar, ever ready to help his fellow man, came to look at the logs. When he saw the tiny stub of a log, he realized they could cut end after end forever, but there would still be no end to two ends.

"There is no need to cut further," he announced. "All you have to do is carry these logs breadthwise into town. That way both ends will be first, and both will be honored equally."

Oyzar's solution had overcome their difficulty, but as soon as the men began to carry the logs, they saw they were faced with still another predicament. The road into town, lined with houses, was far too narrow for the length of the logs.

This time the men took it upon themselves to find a solution. They didn't want Oyzar or anyone else, God forbid, to think of them as fools. They simply tore down the buildings on both sides of the road, then proceeded to carry the logs to the bathhouse site. The houses would have to be rebuilt, of course, but that would have to come later. After all, even angels can't sing two songs at once.

For now, the quandary of which end of the logs to honor had been resolved.

EVENTUALLY the *mikva* was completed, and a lovely bathhouse it was. Only the most polished stones from the river were used to line the sides of the men's and women's tubs. Rich red tiles from Kuzmer covered the roof, and set high in the walls were thick beveled windows from Bialystok through which the rays of the afternoon sun became a thousand rainbows that danced on the pools below.

Everything was in place except the benches. They still had to be built, and it was about these unbuilt benches that a discussion began. The discussion became a debate and the debate became a dispute, because there were some who thought the benches should be smooth while others thought they should be rough.

The smoothniks, as they were called, claimed that if the benches weren't sanded smooth, everyone would leave the bathhouse with tiny splinters in their you-know-whats, and that would never do.

That might be true, agreed the roughniks, as the opposition was called, but a few splinters would be much less harmful than the slipping and sliding that was sure to occur if the benches were sanded smooth. Once the wood got wet, and there was no question that it would get wet in a bathhouse, the benches would become as slick as fresh ice, and the slipping and sliding would begin.

When people slip and slide, someone's sure to fall, and when someone falls, someone's bound to bump his head, and when someone bumps his head, someone's likely to get knocked out, and if someone is knocked out, someone's probably not going to wake up, and if someone doesn't wake up, it'll mean that someone has died, and if someone dies, it'd be a far greater tragedy than having a few people walk around with splinters in their you-know-whats.

"Ridiculous," countered the smoothniks. "The benches in every bathhouse in the world are smooth."

"This bathhouse is not every bathhouse," countered the roughniks. "This is Chelm's bathhouse."

And so the dispute went, back and forth, back and forth, until a compromise was reached: the benches were properly sanded, but to keep people from slipping and sliding they were set with the smooth side down.

Pinkhes the Peddler

There lived in Chelm a man who spent as much time away from his home as he did at it. His name was Pinkhes, and he was a peddler by trade. He would travel to all the surrounding towns and villages, offering his wares for sale.

"Pots and pans," he would call out. "Pots and pans for sale," and everyone would know the peddler had arrived. His sack was always filled to overflowing, and not just with pots and pans. There would be cups and dishes, spools of thread, bolts of cloth, even a piece of used clothing now and then. For the young girls there were bits of brightly colored ribbon and amber beads from the Baltic Sea. For the boys there were spinning tops or maybe a tiny carved wooden bear Pinkhes had picked up somewhere in the dark forests of the Ukraine.

Sometimes Pinkhes traveled in a rickety wagon that squeaked and creaked. It was pulled by a broken-down horse who also squeaked and creaked, but sometimes the horse was too weak or too hungry or too dead to go anywhere. On those days Pinkhes would fill his sack with as much as he could carry and set off on foot.

Once he was trudging home after selling hardly anything when a kindhearted farmer stopped and offered him a ride in his hay-filled wagon.

Pinkhes politely accepted the offer, climbed up on the wagon, and sat down beside the farmer, all the time keeping his sack slung over his shoulder. The farmer giddyapped his horse, and off they went.

A mile down the road, Pinkhes still had not put down his sack. The farmer thought it odd but said nothing. He figured his passenger would do so once he felt at ease, but after a few more miles Pinkhes still had his heavy sack hanging over his back.

Unable to contain himself any longer, the farmer asked, "Why don't you put your sack down in the wagon? Surely you'd be more comfortable that way."

"You're probably right," answered Pinkhes, "but I also have a horse and know how hard they must work, poor creatures. Your horse is kind enough to carry me, and I'm grateful. I wouldn't want to add my load to his burden."

PINKHES THE PEDDLER was a popular fellow in Chelm, not so much for the things he sold (just about all of it could be found in one shop or another), but because he brought back news of the outside world. With few exceptions, most Chelmites spent their lives close to Chelm, but Pinkhes was always crossing rivers and mountains that most townsfolk had never heard of, never mind seen.

Returning from one of his trips, Pinkhes announced that a traveling circus was heading toward Chelm. The children had never been to a circus. Just the idea of seeing a real tiger or a camel was enough to set their heads spinning.

However, that dream was not to be, because Pinkhes also declared that under no circumstances should such a circus be allowed in Chelm.

When the children asked why, he said, "They were unkind, meanspirited, and anti-Semitic. Why, they called me all sorts of terrible names, names I wouldn't dare repeat lest my tongue turn to stone."

"Well, what did you do?" a little girl asked.

"I got my revenge," he said proudly. "I bought a ticket and I didn't go in."

ONCE, at the approach of the Sabbath, Pinkhes found himself in Berdichev. He was a long way from home, and even if he'd had two fleet-footed stallions harnessed to his wagon instead of his old nag, he never would have reached Chelm in time to welcome the Sabbath angels with his family. He decided to spend the night where he was.

He arrived at the Berdichev synagogue a little early and stood by the stove, warming himself while he waited for the evening prayers to begin. The *shammes* noticed him and, wanting to make this stranger feel comfortable, engaged him in conversation.

"Do you like riddles?" he asked.

"Oh, I love riddles," answered Pinkhes.

"Well, here's one for you," said the *shammes*. "Who am I? I am my father's son, but I am not my brother."

"That's it?" Pinkhes asked.

"That's it."

"I am my father's son, but I am not my brother. I am my father's son, but I am not my brother. I am my father's son, but I am not my brother," Pinkhes repeated again and again.

He stretched his mind as far as it would go, but no solution presented itself. "All right," he said, "I give up. Who is it?"

"Why, it's me!" announced the *shammes*.

Ah, what a wonderful riddle, thought the peddler. He was delighted with its cleverness and could scarcely wait to share it with his friends back in Chelm.

When he returned home a few days later, he wasted no time. He assembled his fellow Sages and told them, "I have a wonderful riddle for you, but it is very difficult, so difficult, in fact, I doubt whether even your combined wisdom can answer it. Are you ready?"

"We're ready. We're ready."

"Here it is. I am my father's son, but I am not my brother. Who am I?"

First there was a silence, then a murmur, finally a steady drone as if a hive of bees had just entered the room. "I am my father's son, but I am not my brother. I am my father's son, but I am not my brother," the Sages repeated. Brows were scrunched, eyes were squinted, fingers were pointed at temples as they went on reciting the riddle. "I am my father's son, but I am not my brother. I am my father's son, but I am not my brother."

Again and again and again the riddle was intoned until finally, in unison, they said, "We give up. Tell us. Who is it?"

"Why, it's the *shammes* at the Berdichev synagogue," Pinkhes said triumphantly. "And," he added, "if you don't believe me, I can have him come here and tell you himself."

PINKHES once traded a batch of his own goods for a load of oats, which he drove to the marketplace in his wagon.

A merchant approached and asked, "What are you selling today?"

Pinkhes looked behind him at his horse and wagon, covered his hand with his mouth, and whispered softly into the merchant's ear, "Oats."

"Oats?" asked the man, surprised. "If you're selling oats, why does it have to be a secret?"

"Shh, shh," whispered Pinkhes. "Not so loud, please. I don't want my horse to know."

Yossel and Sossel

Chelm was not the wealthiest town in the world. Oh, there were rich men, but none to brag about as you might about a Rothschild or a Rockefeller, and because even a peeled

grape does not fall into your mouth without help, everyone had to work—whether they wanted to or not.

Some men were forced to seek employment in the neighboring towns and cities beyond the valley. Most found work close enough so they could return to their homes and families each week to observe the Sabbath. Most, that is, but not Yossel.

Yossel, whose family had grown to five children, took a position teaching others' children in Kotsk. Kotsk was less than half a day's journey from Chelm; yet Yossel returned home only once a year. That was each spring, when he came back to Chelm to celebrate the eight days of Passover.

Because family life is such a treasure, the teacher's continual absence troubled the rabbi. It didn't seem right that a man should be separated from his wife and children for most of the year. He called Yossel to him and asked him about the situation.

"Yossel, dear Yossel, there is something about your life that disturbs me deeply."

"But, Rabbi, what could disturb you? It was you who told me that teaching is an honorable profession."

"True, Yossel, true. The teaching of children is as important as any prayer. That is not what bothers me. It is the fact that you come home to your own children and your wife only once a year. It's not as if you were working in another country. You're close enough to join your family every *Shabbes*."

"Every *Shabbes*?" Yossel protested. "Rabbi, you don't realize what it is you're asking me to do. Every *Pesach* I come home, and every *Chanukah*, nine months later, my wife has another baby. Do you know what would happen if I came home every week?"

AFTER THE RABBI's elucidation, and his own consideration, Yossel saw the truth of his situation. He followed the rabbi's counsel and acquired a teaching position in Chelm.

One autumn, shortly after *Yom Kippur*, he went to visit some of his relatives in Dubno, across the Bug River. He hadn't been gone a week when a messenger brought Sossel this letter:

> *Greetings to my wonderful wife.*
> *All is well so far, and I pray the same is true for you. The cold autumn winds are beginning to blow here. I send this letter because I want you to send me your slippers. I say your slippers*

instead of my slippers, because if I said my slippers, you would read my slippers and send me your slippers, and that would never do because I would end up with your slippers and you would end up with my slippers, and one pair would be too big and one pair would be too small. Therefore, I say your slippers so that you'll read your slippers and send me my slippers. I greet the children and send my blessings.

Your faithful husband,

Yossel

Sossel read the letter only once and immediately sent Yossel his slippers, proving, not that anyone ever doubted it, that the women of Chelm were equal in their wisdom to their men.

Shortly after his return from Dubno, Yossel was sitting at the kitchen table writing a letter by the light of a single kerosene lamp. Sossel joined him and noticed that he was making unusually large letters, so large, in fact, that he could fit no more than a few words on each sheet of paper.

"Who are you writing to?" she asked.

"My uncle in Dubno."

"But why are you making such large letters?"

"Because," answered Yossel, "may it never happen to you or me, he's deaf."

"I'm sorry he's deaf, but what does that have to do with the size of the letters?"

"Oh, he can't read," Yossel explained, "so whoever reads this to him will know to read it loud enough so he'll be able to hear."

Berish the Shammes

As the caretaker of the synagogue, Berish the *Shammes* stood at the center of communal life. He was not only expected to keep the synagogue clean and the prayer books and ceremonial objects

in good repair, he was also responsible for keeping the heat in and the rain out.

When a sundial was donated and a rainstorm drenched it, it was Berish who built a roof to cover it so the dial wouldn't be ruined by getting wet.

But his responsibilities went far beyond maintenance and cleaning. It was Berish who announced the time for prayer each day and the time of the Sabbath bath each week. He collected synagogue dues, carried messages for the rabbi, and, in the end, made everyone's funeral arrangements.

Once there was a dreadful accident in the marketplace. Meyer the Driver had gotten his wagon stuck deeply in the mud. Just as his horse was pulling it free, Meyer slipped under the wheels and was killed instantly.

His wife, Rifke, had to be told, so the rabbi turned to his trusted aide for this delicate task.

"Berish," he instructed him, "I want you to go to Rifke and tell her that her husband has been killed, but I want you to break the news to her as gently as possible. Do you understand?"

"Don't worry, Rabbi," Berish assured him. "I'll be as gentle as a mother with a newborn baby."

The *shammes* set off immediately for Meyer's house. He knocked, and a woman came to the door.

"Good afternoon. Could you tell me if the Widow Rifke lives here?" he asked.

"I'm Rifke and I live here," she replied, "but I'm not a widow."

"Ho, ho, ho," chuckled Berish. "How much do you want to bet?"

ONE OF Berish's weekly tasks was to walk through Chelm each Friday afternoon, just before the sun began to set, alerting all the merchants that it would soon be time for them to close their shops and prepare for the Sabbath.

It happened that one Friday, early in the winter, the first snow fell. It began late in the morning and continued well into the afternoon. By the time it stopped, it seemed as if the entire town had been wrapped in a white prayer shawl. The snow covered the muddy, rutted streets and the smoke-stained roofs of the houses. Everything looked so fresh and new it dazzled the eye.

The rabbi, taking a rest from his studies, was gazing out the window at the sparkling landscape when a disturbing thought jolted him from his reverie. It would soon be time for Berish to make his rounds. To do so, he would have to tread upon the pure snow, leaving dirty tracks behind him wherever he went.

The rabbi's love and appreciation of natural beauty ran so deep that he wanted everyone else in Chelm to enjoy it also. What to do? What to do?

Another problem—but to the rabbi such matters were like a loaf of freshly baked pumpernickel to a starving man. He simply rested his elbows on his desk, scrunched up his brow, squinted his eyes, pointed his index finger at his temple, and thought.

Even before a hungry man could devour that loaf, the rabbi knew what must be done to keep the *shammes* from marring the beauty of the newly fallen snow. Berish should stand on a table so his feet would not disturb so much as a flake. Then four strong men would each grab a leg and carry the table with Berish on it throughout the town.

So well did this plan work that, to the delight of all true lovers of beauty, it became one of Chelm's most enduring traditions.

OLD AGE comes to us all and so it did to Berish. As he began to lose his hair, he also began to lose some of his strength. He was no longer robust as he had once been, and it became more and more difficult for him to trudge through the streets of town each day, banging on the shutters to call the people to morning prayers.

As soon as the situation came to the rabbi's attention, he knew that something had to be done. To ask Berish to continue with this task would be most unkind, but to replace him with someone else would be more than unkind. It would be an insult, since no one likes to be told they're too old to do what they did only yesterday.

In the end it was the rabbi's infinite wisdom, kindness, and loyalty to his *shammes* that led to the solution: henceforth, all the shutters from all the houses would be stored in the synagogue courtyard, where Berish could bang them without straining himself by having to walk around the town.

A Celebration

When little Esther was born, her father, Reb Gershon, one of Chelm's most prosperous merchants, was filled with joy and swelled with pride. To celebrate the birth of his first daughter,

he invited, not only his immediate family and closest friends, but also the most eminent citizens of Chelm. "Please come and eat and be merry in honor of my daughter, Esther," said the invitation.

His house was crowded with guests. The tables were covered with snow-white linen cloths, and on the tables were dozens of jugs of water, a dozen dozen at least, surrounded by hundreds of crystal glasses.

Reb Gershon greeted everyone. Everyone congratulated him. Some brought gifts for Esther. People talked politely with one another while they waited for the feast to begin. They talked and waited and talked some more, until it became clear that nothing but water would be served.

One of the elders finally took it upon himself to ask, "Reb Gershon, what's going on here? You invite us to a feast to celebrate your daughter's birth, and all you're serving is water? What kind of a feast is that?"

"But water's the very best thing I could possibly serve," Reb Gershon replied proudly.

When he saw the blank stares on everyone's face, he continued, "You see, I had decided that nothing would be too good for this feast, so yesterday I went to the fish market and asked for the finest fish available. The fishmonger said, 'I have some fish here that are as sweet as sugar,' so I thought to myself that sugar must be better than fish.

"I went to the grocer and asked for sugar, and he boasted that his sugar was as sweet as honey, so naturally I assumed that honey would be better than sugar. I asked for honey, and he told me that his was as pure as olive oil.

"Well, I figured that oil must be better than honey, so

I asked if he had any. Just as he started to fill a bottle, he assured me, 'This oil pours like water.' I didn't need anyone to convince me that water must certainly be better than oil.

"I mean, since sugar is better than fish, and honey is better than sugar, and oil is better than honey, and water is better than oil, then water must be the very best of all. And since all of you have honored me by coming here to celebrate the birth of my daughter, should I insult you by serving anything less than the best?"

No one could dispute such remarkable reasoning, and everyone raised their water-filled crystal glasses in a joyous toast, "*L'chayim!* To life! To Esther!"

The Inn of the Stolen Moon

On the eastern edge of Chelm,
just inside the gate, beside
the road that leads out into the world and
back again, stands a large, rambling, two-story
wooden building. Behind it is a group of sheds

and stables, each one of which leans crazily in its own direction, and in front, hanging from a pine post, is a sign so faded that it can be read only if the person reading it already knows what it says.

THE INN OF THE TWO BROTHERS, proclaims the sign, and although it's true that the brothers Avrom and Reuven are its owners, everyone in Chelm calls the place THE INN OF THE STOLEN MOON. Let me explain.

Avrom and Reuven wanted to be rich. Actually it was more that they were tired of being poor. As is the case with many poor dreamers, not only in Chelm but throughout the world, the brothers spent more time thinking about work than doing it, the result of which was, they remained poor.

For example, they once considered selling bagels, but that would mean baking them, and baking them, as any baker can testify, means work. Baking bagels was out of the question. They thought they'd found an easy way to riches when Avrom suggested that, instead of selling the bagels themselves, they sell the holes that go in the middle of the bagels.

"Every bagel baker needs holes. A bagel without a hole is no bagel at all," he proclaimed.

Reuven agreed wholeheartedly. "Without a hole, a bagel is just a roll."

Try as they might, however, they could not discover a source for the holes, and that proposal, like so many others, had to be abandoned.

IT WAS an earlier and far more ambitious scheme, however, that had changed the name of the inn in everyone's mind from The Inn of the Two Brothers to The Inn of the Stolen Moon.

Avrom and Reuven knew that, during *Rosh Chadosh* at the beginning of every month, in villages and towns like their own, Jews observed a special ceremony to welcome the new moon. When the first slim silver crescent reappeared after nights lit only by stars, the people would leave the synagogue, go into the fields, and say the Blessing of the New Moon.

It was a practice that had been followed for as long as anyone could remember, and was as important a part of everyone's life as the lighting of the candles each week to welcome the Sabbath.

Without the moon, reasoned the brothers (and who could argue?), the blessing would be impossible. If someone could capture the moon and keep it in Chelm, then Jews from all over the world would have to travel to Chelm in order to perform the ceremony. If that someone who now owned the moon were to charge a small fee to use the moon, a fee that even a beggar could afford, say a *zloty* or two, then each month those *zlotys* would be sure to add up to a substantial sum.

And further, if that someone also happened to own the only inn in Chelm (as did the brothers—"Aha!"), the only place visitors could stay and take their meals, then that someone would soon be wealthy beyond measure.

After such a brilliant analysis of the situation, all that remained was for Avrom and Reuven to make this dream a reality. Although they preferred idleness and leisure to actual labor, the promise of such great wealth was so alluring, the brothers wasted no time in putting their plan into action.

Now, the moon, especially when it's full, loves water. Whenever the full moon is out and about on its journey across the heavens, it always stops to refresh itself in bodies of water: ponds, lakes, streams, quiet eddies in a river, even the countless mud puddles that mark the roads in spring and fall. The moon never fails to visit them all—if only for a moment. As they say in Chelm, "Even a blind man can see that."

All the brothers had to do was create their own body of water, one that could be sealed tight, so when the moon came to visit, it couldn't escape.

Dovid the Barrelmaker supplied the barrel, complete with a lid, and Simon the Water Carrier filled it with water from his buckets. Avrom and Reuven had what they needed. It seemed that capturing the moon was going to be as simple as eating honey with a spoon on a hot summer day.

The brothers said nothing to anyone, not wanting to share their perfect plan, or their perfect profits. They hid the barrel in one of the old, unused sheds behind the inn and waited patiently for the full moon to return to Chelm.

It wasn't long before the moon appeared in all its glory. The brothers were ready. They dragged the barrel outside and removed its lid. They themselves hid quietly in the shadows, holding their breath, not daring to speak, lest the moon become suspicious and run away before it could be captured.

Slowly the moon glided through the night sky, bathing the world below in its cool, soft glow. When it was directly above the barrel, it dropped into the water to take a sip. Avrom and Reuven rushed forward, covered the barrel with the lid, and nailed it shut so the moon had no way out.

All had gone according to their plan. The moon was theirs. Soon they would be rich men.

A few days before the beginning of the month of *Tammuz*, the brothers started spreading word that they now owned the moon, but being of generous natures, they'd be willing to make it available to anyone—for a small rental fee, of course. When the other Chelmites heard about this, they thought it must be some kind of joke they couldn't understand, a riddle perhaps. Who ever heard of anyone owning the moon? But all Avrom and Reuven would say was, "You'll see. You'll see," as they went on dreaming of the day their fortunes were to change forever.

The month of *Sivan* ended and the month of *Tammuz* arrived, finally *Rosh Chadosh* was at hand, but no one came to rent the moon—no one from Chelm, no one from Kotz in the north or Belz in the south, no one at all. What did come, just as it always has and always will, was the new crescent moon, and the good folk of Chelm went out into the fields, already thick with barley, to give thanks and say the Blessing of the New Moon.

"Something's gone wrong," Avrom suggested, trying to keep out of his voice the panic that was swiftly settling in his mind.

"What could go wrong?" asked Reuven, still convinced their plan would work. "There's only one true moon, and we have it locked up. That one in the sky must be an impostor."

"You're probably right," Avrom agreed, "but we'd better check just to be sure."

The brothers gathered up their hammers and crowbar and went out to the shed where they'd hidden the barrel.

"Be careful when you open the lid," Avrom cautioned. "We don't want to let it get away."

They pried the lid off slowly and with great care, ready to grab the moon if it should try to flee, but when they looked, there was nothing to be seen, only the water that filled the barrel.

"Maybe it sank to the bottom," Reuven offered, with only the slightest glimmer of hope in his voice.

"Let's hope so," Avrom said with a sigh, hoping but not really believing.

They tilted the barrel and poured out the water bit by bit, but there was no sign of the moon—not in the water, not in the barrel, not on the ground.

"It's been stolen!" screamed Avrom.

"It's been stolen!" Reuven joined in.

"Someone stole our moon! Someone stole our moon!" they shouted and cried together.

All this flurry and fuss brought people running. The brothers were hysterical, but eventually they calmed down enough to explain what had happened. They revealed their plan to steal the moon, but instead some scoundrel had stolen it from them.

Now the people of Chelm understood what the brothers had been babbling about when they said they'd be willing to rent the moon. It wasn't a joke or a riddle at all. It was just one more of Avrom and Reuven's never-ending schemes to get rich.

And from that night on, their inn became known as The Inn of the Stolen Moon, and it will continue to be called that as long as angels have wings.

Reuven's wife, Raisela, was not a dreamer like her husband or her brother-in-law, Avrom. She was practical and orderly, so it was she who took care of most of the business of running the inn.

Raisela was also responsible for the kitchen. She was known far and wide for her culinary skills. In other words, she was a marvelous cook. Her brisket and roast chicken were beyond compare, and her *kugel* and *kreplach* and *tsimmes* were, some said, a taste of Paradise.

Once a lumber merchant traveling to the fir forests of the north stopped at the inn to partake of one of Raisela's meals, and a grand feast it was. When he had finished, he called for the bill so he might be on his way.

"Let's see," said Raisela, "the matzah ball soup, the chopped liver, and the bread come to seven *zlotys*. The roast chicken, the *tsimmes*, and the *helzel*, oh, and let's not forget the honey cakes and tea, come to another seven *zlotys*, which altogether totals eleven *zlotys*."

"I beg your pardon," the lumber merchant said politely, "but seven and seven are fourteen."

"No," insisted Raisela, "seven and seven are eleven."

"Madam, that was such a magnificent meal, one that I'll not soon forget, I wouldn't want to cheat you out of what's rightfully yours. I'll pay you whatever you ask, but where I come from, two times seven are fourteen, not eleven."

"Maybe where you come from it's fourteen," Raisela said, "but here seven and seven are eleven, and I'll prove it to you. My first husband, may he rest in peace, died five years ago, leaving me a widow with four children. Reuven's wife, may she also rest in peace, also died around that time, leaving him a widower with four children. Sheyne-Lieba, the *shadchen*, the matchmaker, introduced us and we married. Then we were blessed with three children of our own. Now each of us has seven children, and together we have eleven children. So you see, seven and seven are eleven, and that's what you owe me for your meal."

The lumber merchant said nothing further (what could he say?), paid his bill, and continued on his journey to the north. Once again Chelmic logic had triumphed over that of the rest of the world.

Elders and Riddlers

Faivel and Fishel were two of the most respected elders of Chelm. Experienced both in the ways of the world and the ways of wisdom, they each had lived many years and done many things.

Faivel had been a baker and Fishel a tailor, but now that they each had grandchildren and great-grandchildren, their days of labor were behind them.

Much of their time was spent in the Tea House. There they would sit for hours on end, sipping tall glasses of blackberry tea, philosophizing and discussing the state of the world.

"I don't understand," Faivel wondered aloud one day, "why the government makes life so difficult for the poor by taking their last coins for taxes."

"The government needs taxes. Every government collects taxes—always has, always will," Fishel explained.

"But," continued Faivel, "why must the government collect from us? It has a mint of its own. Why can't it simply make as many *zlotys* as it needs?"

"Oh, it could, it could," said Fishel, "but it's just like God and the angels."

"God and the angels? What are you talking about, Reb Fishel?"

"You know, Reb Faivel, that every time a human being does a good deed he creates an angel. Now, God could create all the angels he wants, but he doesn't do so. Why doesn't he? I'll tell you why. He would rather have your angel than his own. It's the same with taxes. Of course the government could produce as many *zlotys* as it likes, but it would much rather have yours."

ON ANOTHER OCCASION it was Fishel who came up with the question of the day. "Why is it," he asked, "that every time you clean something, something else gets dirty? Whereas whenever you make something dirty, nothing ever gets clean?"

Since neither he nor his fellow philosopher were able to unravel the mystery—not even after three glasses of tea—they decided to set out on their daily stroll.

It was a bright afternoon in the middle of summer, but Faivel was carrying an umbrella. Since the sky was as blue as a thousand robins' eggs, Fishel thought the umbrella a little odd. However, Faivel was an eminent Sage like himself, so surely he must have a good reason.

Suddenly, as if out of nowhere, dark clouds filled the sky and it began to rain.

"Quick," said Fishel, "put up your umbrella."

"It wouldn't do any good," answered Faivel.

"What do you mean, it wouldn't do any good? It's raining cats and dogs."

"It could rain whales and elephants. It still wouldn't do any good. My umbrella's full of holes."

"It's full of holes? Then why did you bring it?"

"I didn't think it would rain," Faivel said.

THE DOWNPOUR went as quickly as it came, and Faivel and Fishel continued their stroll through the countryside. They had paused to rest beside a green field where a milk cow was tethered when Faivel slapped his forehead and exclaimed, "Oy! I think I've found a flaw in creation."

"A flaw in creation?" asked his friend incredulously. "What could possibly be wrong with creation?"

"Well," explained Faivel, "take that cow and the birds. Just have a look. The birds are so tiny and their needs are so small—yet God has given them wings so they are able to partake of the bounties of the sky as well as the earth. But the cow, the cow is immense and her needs are great—yet she is bound to the earth. Why didn't God give the cow wings?"

Just then a flock of birds flew directly overhead. One of them responded to the call of nature—*splat!*—right on Faivel's head. He looked up and said, "Aha, I think I know why."

AS YOU MIGHT EXPECT, Faivel and Fishel were, like most philosophers, expert riddlers. One of Faivel's favorites was *What do you have that other people use more than you do?*

And a favorite of Fishel's was *What do you have that goes all over the room and never touches anything?*

Actually, these riddles and others like them were favorites among both children and adults because, no matter how difficult they seem at first, it was always possible, with enough thought, to figure out the answer.

OYZAR THE SCHOLAR was also a riddler of some note, but his riddles usually made sense *only* after they were explained. Although everyone respected Oyzar for his unique scholarship, there were a few who suggested he spent too much of his time dreaming and that this may have had something to do with the peculiarity of his riddles.

An example: *Why does the dog wag its tail?*
Oyzar's answer: *Because the dog is stronger than the tail. Otherwise, the tail would wag the dog.*

Or: *Why does the hair on a man's head turn gray before the hair in his beard?*

The answer: *Because the hair on his head is at least twenty years older than the hair in his beard.*

Oyzar's own favorite was more complicated.

"What," he would ask, "is green and whistles and hangs on the wall?"

No one was ever able to figure out the answer.

Oyzar, chuckling into his beard—by that time grown long and white—would proclaim, "Why, a herring!"

"A herring?" people would ask in astonishment. "A herring isn't green."

"You could paint it green."

"But a herring doesn't hang on the wall," they argued.

"If you wanted to, you could hang it," explained Oyzar.

"But, but," they would stutter in protest, "there's never been a herring that whistled and there never will be."

"Oh"—Oyzar would laugh triumphantly—"I just threw that in to make it hard."

Oyzar used to ask one even *he* had no answer for: *Why is it that if there's a hole in your shoe, water runs in, but if there's a hole in your pot, the water runs out?*

OH, YOU'VE PROBABLY FIGURED OUT the answers to Faivel's and Fishel's favorite riddles, but just in case . . .

What you have that others use more than you do is your name, and what you have that goes all over the room without touching anything is your voice.

The Feather Merchants

Chelm woke one winter morning to find itself covered in white. It had snowed all through the night and was snowing still. Everything was buried, and no one was going anywhere. Heaven and earth seemed joined together.

Avrom and Reuven sat alone in the main room of the empty inn gazing at the fire, dreaming about the old, waiting for the new. Their most recent venture into the world of commerce had been a true disaster, although neither would admit it.

Months before, at the beginning of autumn, Raisela gave her husband Reuven a large (large for her, at least) sum of money that she had painstakingly saved. She sent him off to the weekly market in Lublin to buy some new pots and pans, some utensils she needed for the kitchen.

It was only natural that Avrom should accompany his brother to the big city, and, as they traveled, it was also only natural that they began to discuss ways they might take that money and turn it into even more.

"What does Raisela need new pots and pans for?" Avrom asked. "She's already the finest cook in all of Chelm. Will new pans make her a better cook?"

"I suppose not," said Reuven, "but she did ask for them, so she must have a good reason."

"I'm sure she does. I'm sure she does," Avrom agreed, "but she doesn't need them today or even tomorrow, does she? Her food will taste just as sweet if she cooks a few more meals in the old pots. If we can invest this money in something and then sell that something for more than we paid for it, we'll have plenty for Raisela's pots and pans and more besides, and with that more we'll be on our way to becoming the rich men we were born to be."

It sounded like a fine idea to Reuven, so when the brothers arrived in Lublin they immediately went to the marketplace, seeking something they could buy low and sell high.

They considered stoves. Winter would soon be here, and everyone needed a stove, but on second thought stoves would be far too heavy to carry back to Chelm.

Anvils? Anvils were heavy but much, much lighter than stoves. On third thought, however, no one but blacksmiths used anvils, and Chelm's only blacksmith, Zabalye, already owned three. No, anvils were also out.

The brothers went from stall to stall, shop to shop, store to store. They looked at what the peasants had brought to market in their carts and wagons, all with little success until Reuven called out, "I have it. I have it. We'll buy pillows."

"Pillows? Why pillows?" asked Avrom.

"Well, first of all, pillows are light, certainly lighter than anvils or stoves," Reuven explained. "And besides, who has not heard the saying 'Sleep faster; we need the pillows.' "

"Which must mean," Avrom said excitedly, "that there are simply not enough pillows to go around."

"Exactly the point."

And so the brothers took all of Raisela's pots-and-pans money and invested it in pillows, dozens and dozens and dozens of pillows. Reuven was right about pillows being light, but they are also fluffy, bulky, and unwieldy, particularly if they have to be carried any distance. A man might be able to carry four or five himself or, if he planned meticulously, ten or so strapped to his back, but dozens upon dozens were out of the realm of possibility, as was hiring a wagon to carry them back to Chelm, since they'd spent their very last *zloty* filling out their collection with a tiny pillow for a baby.

There they sat on the edge of the Lublin market with their towering pile of pillows.

The sun was going down in the west. The color of the sky changed from robins' eggs to roses to ashes; a breeze began to blow. Soon it would be dark, and it seemed another of the brothers' schemes was destined for failure. But then the breeze billowed into a wind which blew, of all places, in the direction of Chelm.

At that moment Reuven had another brilliant idea. "There's really no need for *us* to carry these pillows. All we have to do is cut them open and let the wind carry the feathers back to Chelm. Then we gather them up, make them into pillows again, and we'll be rich."

Avrom marveled at his brother's wisdom. Two radiantly remarkable ideas in a single day. This would indeed be a day long remembered in their family history.

They did not hesitate. They slit open the pillows, even the tiny baby one, and cast every last feather into the air, absolutely sure that they'd be borne back to Chelm by the wind.

When the brothers arrived home two days later, the first thing they did was to ask Raisela, "Where did you put all our feathers?"

"Feathers? What feathers?" she asked in return. "What are you babbling about now? And where are my pots and pans?"

Reuven explained their pillow plan as best he could and tried to calm her with promises of untold riches and more pots and pans than she could use in a lifetime, but Raisela was far too wise and far too experienced to pin her hopes on a whirlwind of feathers flying around God knows where. They could be halfway to America or all the way across Russia for all anyone knew. Pillows indeed!

But Avrom and Reuven were certain the feathers would appear.

"Look," Avrom said, "it took us two days to walk from Lublin. It probably takes a feather even longer, especially one that's never been here before."

"If a man can get lost, then surely a feather can lose its way," Reuven added.

Day after day they waited. There was no sign of their feathers, not even a speck of down.

"Could they have been stolen? No. A moon can be

stolen. A pillow can be stolen. But zillions and zillions of feathers? Never."

"Perhaps the wind stopped to rest. Perhaps it grew tired carrying all those feathers."

Perhaps, but when the Sabbath came and went, the brothers felt they had to do something. Each day they walked to the outskirts of Chelm to await their feathers and their fortune. They even put signs up along the road:

FEATHERS! → THIS WAY TO AVROM AND REUVEN

Weeks passed. Months. *Rosh Hashanah, Yom Kippur, Succoth.* The leaves of the oak turned from green to gold and began to fall to the ground. The apples were picked and packed away in straw-filled barrels. Only a few still hung on the trees along the orchards' edges, left there for any beggars or wanderers who might pass by. The grain and potatoes, the beets and cabbages had been harvested and stored in root cellars.

And still not a single hint of a single feather.

Now winter was upon them, and as the snow continued to fall, Avrom and Reuven sat side by side, silently staring into the fire, each thinking his own thoughts, which, not surprisingly, were the same thoughts: *Maybe the feathers are buried under the snow. Maybe they're hibernating like the bears. Maybe they'll come in the spring.*

Maybe. Maybe not. The last I heard, Avrom and Reuven were still waiting with perfect faith and hope for their feathers to arrive and make them rich.

And who knows? Perhaps someday they will.

The Council of Seven Sages

B y now it should be clear that everyone in Chelm
was steeped in the ways of wisdom.
Yet wise as Chelmites were, a special group of
Sages was needed to guide the community through

the *most* perplexing problems and quandaries. When the rabbi had no answer, when Oyzar the Scholar could not come up with a solution, when those most respected elders, Faivel and Fishel, were unable to unravel the complexities of the situation, the people always turned to the Council of Seven Sages—the wisest of the wise, one for each day of the week.

For example, when the question was raised, which is more important, the sun or the moon, all of Chelm divided into two camps. Those who felt the sun was more important were just as passionate as those who felt the moon was more important. Households opposed households, husbands argued with wives, children disagreed with their parents. Just as the entire community was about to come to blows, the Council of Seven Sages took the question under consideration. That was, after all, what they were there for.

For seven days and seven nights the Council met and pondered. They discussed, deliberated, and dissected the question and finally announced their decision: clearly it was the moon, because the moon shines at night when we need the light the most, whereas the sun shines during the day when we already have plenty of light.

THE COUNCIL was also able, after much musing, to clear up a mystery that has baffled great minds for centuries—that is, why is it cold in the winter and hot in the summer?

Once again, the problem was so complex the Council needed seven days and seven nights before they could present their answer to the rest of the community with absolute confidence.

Using their brilliant collective knowledge, they explained that during the winter we light our stoves, which, in turn, heat the air around us. Gradually, all the air gets warmer and warmer until, by the time summer arrives, the air has become very hot.

Naturally, we don't want the air to get any hotter, God forbid, so we stop lighting our stoves. Gradually the air cools down until, by the time winter arrives, the air is freezing. That's when we begin to light our stoves, and the process starts all over again.

ONCE THERE was a murder in Chelm. Yes, a murder, just as they have in Warsaw or Moscow or New York.

It happened like this. Selig the Winemaker drank too much of his own wine and, in a fit of drunken passion, killed a fellow Chelmite.

He was brought before the Council of Seven Sages. There had been many witnesses, and Selig did not deny what he had done, nor did he say anything in his own defense. The Council had no choice but to declare him guilty and sentence him to be hanged.

That seemed to settle the matter until Avrom rose in the courtroom and addressed the Council. "Honorable Sages," he said. "It is true that Selig has committed a terrible crime and his sentence is a proper one. However, the Council has failed to take into account an important practical consideration. Selig is our only winemaker. There is not another one within a hundred miles. If we hang him, where will we get our wine?"

For a moment there was a heavy silence as everyone considered the question. Then, almost in unison, a dozen voices cried, "Indeed, indeed, where will we get our wine?"

Some of the Seven Sages were among those asking the question, so they continued their deliberations until they ultimately came up with a revised verdict.

"Since we have only one winemaker, it would be a great wrong against the community to deprive everyone of his skills. Still, justice must be done, and since we have more than enough cobblers, it is decreed that one of them shall be hanged instead."

As WISE AS the Council of Seven Sages was, there are two questions about which they were never able to come to a consensus, and that remain unsettled to this day.

The first concerns how human beings grow. Do they grow from the head up, or do they grow from the feet down?

Those who favored the feet-down theory presented their own experience of growth as proof. When they were young, they said, the day came when they were given their first pair of long pants. Inevitably the pants were so long they dragged on the ground; but as they grew, some faster than others, the pants kept rising until the bottoms were well above their ankles—which proves conclusively that a human being grows from the feet down.

There were, however, other members of the Council who, with just as much conviction, insisted it's the other way around. They steadfastly maintained that we grow from our heads up and offered equally convincing proof on their behalf.

All you need do, they said, is look carefully at a group of marching soldiers. At the bottom their feet are all the same, on the same level. But when you look at their heads, you'll see that some are higher than others, some lower—which demonstrates that we grow from the head up.

THE OTHER QUESTION that even the deepest thinkers of Chelm were never able to agree on has to do with a simple piece of bread and butter. Butter was considered a special treat, so the children were cautioned to be extra careful whenever they were fortunate enough to receive any. If they dropped a slice of buttered bread, they were warned, it would always fall buttered side down.

This had been an accepted truth in Chelm for as long as anyone could remember, until the youngest three of the Seven Sages decided to look into the matter. They discussed, deliberated, and dissected, not for seven days and seven nights or even seven weeks but for seven months. When they announced their conclusion, it created an uproar.

It was not true, they claimed, that a piece of buttered bread always falls buttered side down. To prove it, they would conduct a public scientific experiment.

The town square was filled with seekers of truth that day. They came from miles around.

The three young Sages mounted a platform especially built for the experiment. It stood above the crowd so everyone would be able to see the demonstration with their own eyes. One of the Sages held the bread and one held the butter while the third held a knife, with which he slowly and deliberately buttered the bread.

Next, Kopel the Candlemaker, an ordinary citizen, was called forward. He was asked to hold the bread with the buttered side facing the blue sky and then to drop it. The crowd was hushed as Kopel took the bread. He held it for a moment. The butter began to melt. He dropped it.

The bread fell buttered side down.

"Aha," shouted the four oldest Sages, who had been standing to the side of the platform. "It fell buttered side down. That proves we were right all along."

"All it proves," responded the would-be scientists, "is that we buttered the wrong side."

EVERY ONCE in a while the Council of Seven Sages would repeat the experiment, but no matter which side the bread fell on some of them would insist that the wrong side had been buttered.

Now that you know how the people of Chelm thought and what makes them so wise, I leave you to answer these two vital questions—about how people grow and about how buttered bread falls—for yourself.

Before you're tempted to say, "But I'm no fool," I would urge you to remember what the good folk of Chelm always said: *If you claim you are not a fool, you only show your ignorance, for is it not written that "the world was delivered into the hands of fools"?*

And *I* ask you, is this not the world?

Afterword

I

FOR AS LONG AS I can remember knowing anything, I remember knowing about Chelm and its silly citizens.

I was a very young boy when I heard my first Chelm stories from my grandfather—may his memory be a blessing. He had come to this country from Lithuania near the end of the last century seeking a better life, a life free from *pogroms*, persecution, and poverty.

He had been a baker's apprentice in Vilna, and he continued to follow the baker's trade here in the United States. He was a fine, fine baker, but what he loved to do most of all was tell stories—all kinds of stories. There were stories about great leaders like Abraham and Moses and stories about courageous heroes and heroines like Judah Maccabee and Queen Esther. He told stories of demons and imps, rabbis and holy men, czars and empresses of the distant and not-so-distant past.

Among his favorites were those about the good and decent folk of Chelm. They soon became favorites of mine also, because not only did I hear them from him but from my mother and father, aunts, uncles, cousins, and teachers as well. Often when I said or did something foolish, at least in the eyes of a grown-up, I was told, "Don't be a *Chelmer chochem*. Don't act like a fool from Chelm."

For me Chelm was as real as Hollywood or Antarctica, Krypton or Metropolis, New Orleans or Oz. Faivel and Fishel were no less a part of my life than the Lone Ranger and Tonto.

As a storyteller I've been telling these tales for decades. Listeners frequently ask where they can find them in print. When I realized there was no single source currently available that captured the delightfully unique character of the Chelmites, I decided it was time to commit these stories to paper.

It would be a simple task, I thought. After all, I knew them well. They've been a part of my life for almost half a century. However, once I began to record them, I discovered that, although I knew the Chelmites and their ways intimately, I really didn't know much about *where* they lived.

Were the mountains around Chelm the same as the mountains I now live in? Were they rough and jagged or had they been worn smooth by thousands of years of snow and rain? What kinds of mushrooms grow in the forests? What birds sing at twilight? There were many questions that could be answered only by going to the places where these stories were born.

It became clear that a journey to Eastern Europe would be necessary to learn about the trees and flowers, to experience sunrises and sunsets, to feel the rain, to walk in the mud.

II

ALMOST EVERY CULTURE has its fools or group of fools who are there to help us laugh when we need to the most. Sometimes it's an individual like Jean Sot in France or Silly Jack in England. Sometimes it's an entire town of fools like Schildburg in Germany or Montieri in Italy. For the Greeks it's Abdera; for the English, Gotham; and for the Jews it's Chelm.

No one knows how long people have been telling stories about the Sages (or Fools) of Chelm. Some folklore scholars say five hundred years, others say longer, but just about everyone agrees that the stories originated and developed in the Yiddish-speaking world of Eastern Europe.

Through the years the borders have changed continually. What was once Poland is now part of Russia. What was once Galicia is now part of Poland. But at one time more than seven million Jews lived in a territory that stretched from the Black Sea in the south to the Baltic Sea in the north, from the plains of Germany in the west to the Caucasus Mountains of Russia in the east.

Eastern Europe was once the inspired, vital center of Jewish life and thought, faith, religion, and culture, flourishing from as early as the tenth century until the Nazis appeared in our own century and tried to destroy it forever.

I went there, I think, without illusions. I was well aware of my people's history. I knew that six million of them, along with millions of others, had been murdered during those brutal years some call World War II and others call the Holocaust. I certainly didn't go expecting to find the living, vibrant world of my grandfathers, but I was not prepared for the total absence and denial of the life that had once been there.

I spent most of my time traveling in Poland, from East Germany to the Ukraine and back again. One branch of my family had lived and worked in and around Warsaw for generations, and there were once, in my own lifetime, three and a half million Jews living in Poland.

Now there are less than three thousand, and they are mostly old and isolated. Signs of Jewish life are almost non-existent. Only a few synagogues still stand. The Jewish cemeteries are difficult, if not impossible, to find; they are generally in the final stages of vanishing, either because of neglect (there's simply no one left to care for them) or, worse, because of anti-Semitic desecrations. The monuments and museums at concentration camps like Majdanek and Treblinka barely mention the fact that so many Jews died there. And in the woods, at places like Belzec and Sobibor, where almost no one ever goes, are mounds of the bones and ashes of the victims, bearing silent witness to the monstrous crimes committed there.

III

THE BROKEN LEG I received at the hands of two thugs along the banks of the romantic and heavily polluted Vistula River in the center of ancient Cracow was not the most important part of my trip, only the most dramatic. Those young hoodlums were, after all, only seeking my money, but the incident

and the six painful days it took me to return home and get proper medical attention have come to symbolize for me the difficulties of the journey *and* of keeping these stories alive.

What began as a simple research trip became a journey of the soul, a return to the self, if you will. It became a deeply moving voyage of discovery, one that, among other things, showed me again how necessary a sense of humor is if we are to do more than survive in this world.

These stories about Chelm have been told by the Jewish people during both good times and terrible times. In the best of times, we're able to laugh together. In the worst of times, the innocent stupidity and sweetness of the Chelmites speaks of a universal quality we all recognize and are able to smile at—if only inwardly, if only for a fleeting second.

And it is this smile that connects us to the past and to the future. It is this smile that keeps us human.

IV

ALONG THE WAY I actually did visit a town called Chelm. It is a lovely place situated, not deep in a valley as is the Chelm of legend, but high in the Lublin Uplands with a sweeping view of the surrounding countryside.

It was late autumn. The maples and oaks were ablaze with their new coats of red and yellow leaves. Each evening at sunset it seemed as if entire hillsides were on fire. Except for the last turnips, most of the crops were safely stored away, while the freshly turned fields waited patiently for the nourishment of the first snows.

Red geraniums, white chrysanthemums, pink hollyhocks, and purple asters filled window boxes and gardens. The woods were alive with mushrooms of every shape, every size, every color. Each morning, mist rose from the forest floor but was gone by the time people left their homes on their way to work or to market.

The first Jewish settlers had arrived there almost a thousand years ago. They came to work in the logging and lumber business made possible by the huge forests to the north and east. Less than fifty years ago there were fifteen thousand Jews living in Chelm, almost half the population, but today, among its seventy thousand inhabitants, there are none, absolutely none. They have all disappeared. Most were brutally murdered at the killing camp called Sobibor, located only thirty miles to the northeast. The few that did survive have long ago moved on to new lives elsewhere.

Only a handful of the old people in Chelm remember, or admit to remembering, their onetime neighbors, and none of them know these stories.

Of course, the Chelm of our stories is not the Chelm that today is known in Poland for its shoes and its cement. It never was, even when it sparkled and teemed with Jewish life. Just as nobody knows when these stories began, no one knows how Chelm came to be known as the town of fools.

Our Chelm is the Chelm of the spirit and imagination that has existed, generation after generation, in the minds and hearts of those who've told and listened to these tales.

Our Chelm is a magical place filled with honest and righteous men and women for whom the idea of defeat passes as quickly as a gaggle of geese flying south.

Our Chelm has "a soul which yearns for beauty, which is full of mercy, which possesses faith, which seeks justice."*

Chelm is where hopes and dreams and laughter go on living—and will go on living as long as you and I go on telling these stories.

STEVE SANFIELD

Montezuma Hill, California
Rosh Hashanah 5751 / Autumn 1990

*Yisroel Aschendorf in *The Commemoration Book of Chelm*. M. Bakalczuk-Felin, ed. Johannesburg: Former Residents of Chelm, 1954.

Glossary

aleph-beys First two letters of the Hebrew/Yiddish alphabet. Same as ABC's.

Bar Mitzvah The ceremony, held in a synagogue, in which a thirteen-year-old boy reaches the status of manhood and assumes the rights and obligations of an adult.

Chanukah The Festival of Lights. An eight-day winter celebration commemorating the rededication of the Temple in Jerusalem by the Maccabees after their victory over Syrian despots in 167 B.C.E.

Chelmer chochem Literally "a Sage, or wise man, of Chelm," but when used sarcastically, it means a fool.

Days of Awe The ten-day period of soul-searching and reflection that begins on Rosh Hashanah and culminates in Yom Kippur.

helzel A delicacy made by stuffing the neck of a goose, chicken, or duck with meal, egg, and spices.

kreplach A dumpling of chopped meat or cheese usually served in soup. Called *wonton* in China.

kugel Noodle or bread pudding generally cooked with raisins.

L'chayim "To life." A popular and traditional toast.

Mazel tov "Good luck." Congratulations.

mikva A ritual bathhouse and a necessary part of traditional communities.

Passover An eight-day spring festival commemorating the exodus of the ancient Hebrew people from their slavery in Egypt.

Pesach "Passover."

pogrom An organized attack or persecution, often officially encouraged, particularly against the Jews.

Purim Festival of Lots marking the triumph over the Persian Haman's plot to exterminate the Jews. Noted for its gaiety, masquerades, and festive meal.

Rosh Chadosh "Head of the Month." First day of each Jewish month.

Rosh Hashanah Jewish New Year. Arrives in the fall, usually in September.

schlemiel A clumsy, inept person. A schlemiel will throw a drowning man a rope—both ends.

Shabbes The Sabbath, the holiest day of the week, traditionally devoted to rest, study, prayer, and family. An island in time when every man and woman can become a king and queen and every boy and girl a prince and princess. Begins at sunset on Friday and ends at sunset on Saturday.

shadchen A professional matchmaker.

shammes The sexton, caretaker of a synagogue; the rabbi's personal attendant.

shul Synagogue. The center of Jewish communal life, where people meet, pray, study, debate, and argue.

Sivan and **Tammuz** The ninth and tenth months, respectively, of the Jewish year. Midsummer.

Succoth An autumn harvest festival.

Talmud "Teaching." A vast record of discussions and commentaries, recorded over many centuries, dealing with law, ethics, traditions, and ceremony.

Torah "The Law." The Pentateuch, or Five Books of Moses, but also refers to the practice and teachings of Judaic law in general.

tsimmes A sweet dish in which carrots, prunes, and/or sweet potatoes are mixed with honey and spices and left to cook slowly for many hours.

Yom Kippur Day of Atonement. The most solemn and sacred day of the year, spent in fasting and prayer.

zloty A large, silver coin, generally worth as little as a penny and as much as a quarter, depending on the time and place of its use.

Bibliography

Should you be interested in seeing how other writers and story-tellers have chosen to tell some of these and other stories of Chelm, the following books in English are recommended.

Ausubel, Nathan, ed. *A Treasury of Jewish Folklore*. New York: Crown Publishers, 1948.

Browne, Lewis. *The Wisdom of Israel*. New York: Random House, 1945. Reprinted as *Wisdom of the Jewish People*. Northvale, N.J.: Jason Aronson, Inc., 1988.

Freedman, Florence B. *It Happened in Chelm: A Story of the Legendary Town of Fools*. New York: Shampolsky Publishers, 1990.

Howe, Irving, and Eliezer Greenberg, eds. *A Treasury of Yiddish Stories*. New York: Viking Press, 1953. Revised and updated edition. New York: Viking Penguin, 1990.

Jagendorf, M. A. *Noodlehead Stories from Around the World*. New York: The Vanguard Press, 1957.

Leach, Maria. *Noodles, Nitwits, and Numskulls*. Cleveland: World Publishing, 1961. Paperback reprint. New York: Dell Yearling, 1979.

Novak, William, and Moshe Waldoks, eds. *The Big Book of Jewish Humor*. New York: Harper & Row, 1981.

Pavlàt, Leo. *Jewish Folktales*. London: Beehive Books, 1986.

Richman, Jacob. *Jewish Wit and Wisdom*. New York: Padres Publishing House, 1952.

———. *Laughs from Jewish Lore*. New York: Hebrew Publishing Company, 1954.

Roskies, Diane K., and David G. Roskies. *The Shtetl Book*. Hoboken, N.J.: KTAV Publishing House, Inc., 1975.

Schwartz, Amy. *Yossel Zissel and the Wisdom of Chelm*. Philadelphia: The Jewish Publication Society, 1986.

Serwer, Blanche Luria. *Let's Steal the Moon: Jewish Tales Ancient and Recent*. Boston: Little, Brown and Company, 1970. Paperback reprint. New York: Shampolsky Publishers, 1987.

Simon, Solomon. *The Wise Men of Chelm and Their Merry Tales*. New York: Behrman House, 1945.

———. *More Wise Men of Chelm and Their Merry Tales*. New York: Behrman House, 1965.

Singer, Isaac Bashevis. *The Fools of Chelm and Their History*. New York: Farrar, Straus & Giroux, 1968.

———. *Stories for Children*. New York: Farrar, Straus & Giroux, 1984.

———. *Zlateh the Goat and Other Stories*. New York: Harper & Row, 1966.

Spaulding, Henry D. *Encyclopedia of Jewish Humor*. New York: Johnathan David Publishers, 1969.

Tenenbaum, Samuel. *The Wise Men of Chelm*. New York: Thomas Yoseloff, Publisher, 1965. Paperback reprint. New York: Collier Books, 1969.

Weinreich, Beatrice Silverman, ed. *Yiddish Folktales*. New York: Pantheon Books / Yivo Institute for Jewish Research, 1988.

CREATURE CROSSING

Betty Levin

Illustrated by Jos. A. Smith

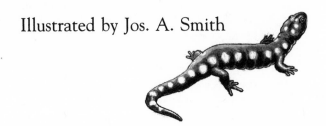

GREENWILLOW BOOKS, New York

The text of this book was set in Goudy O. S.
Printed in the United States of America
First Edition   10 9 8 7 6 5 4 3 2 1

Library of Congress Cataloging-in-Publication Data
Levin, Betty.
Creature crossing / Betty Levin ;
illustrated by Jos. A. Smith.
        p.   cm.
Summary: As they work together to learn about the
creature that Ben had found and to help others like
it to survive, Ben, Kate, and Foster also gain a sense
of their own individual abilities.
ISBN 0-688-16220-7
[1. Salamanders—Fiction.   2. Friendship—Fiction.
3. Wildlife conservation—Fiction.]
I. Smith, Jos. A., ill.   II. Title.
PZ7.L5759Cr   1999   [Fic]—dc21
98-5435   CIP   AC

FOR
JANEY, TIM, TYLER,
AND AMELIA

1 *It was only by accident* that Ben noticed the lizard, or whatever it was. Catching it made him feel like a hunter exposed to unknown risks. It might bite. It could even be poisonous.

First he had to make sure it was alive. Leaning over the ditch, he poked a stick through the pebbles and rattled them all around. Then, gently prodding, he nudged dead, sodden leaves that nearly buried the creature. It didn't stir. It looked a bit like a stick itself, a branch with twigs growing out. Those were its legs and feet.

He almost left it there. Since it wasn't moving, he figured he had plenty of time to get Kate and Foster to come for a look. Only then he would have to share it with them. He didn't usually mind sharing like that. But lately he had had to share too much with his little sister, Daisy. Now that she could run all over the place, including his room, she was into everything.

So Ben decided it would be cool to have something all his own.

It crossed his mind that even if the thing wasn't alive, it might still be special. What if it was a fossil out of a dinosaur egg and millions of years old? He almost hoped it would turn out to be hard as rock. He would let his parents keep it on the mantelpiece for a while to show off to their friends. A reporter might come from the local newspaper to take a picture of it, and everyone in school would know who had found this amazing specimen, previously unknown to science. The newspaper headline would read: YOUNG EXPLORER DISCOVERS FOSSIL DINOSAUR HATCHLING.

Ben had to lie on his stomach to reach whatever it was. Although a few roadside weeds were turning green, the ground was hard and cold, as if still in the grip of winter. Snow had trickled down and then frozen overnight. Ben's hands were so icy when he finally scooped up the motionless creature that he could hardly feel it. Still, he made a bowl of his hands to cover it. Then he raised two fingers to peek inside just to make sure it was really there.

Was it his imagination, or had it curved itself into a semicircle? He couldn't be sure that his own hands hadn't reshaped it. Examining it, he was sorry not to see more of a dinosaur look about it. Its most vivid feature was the yellow spots on its nearly black body.

Cupping it in his hands, Ben set off for Kate's house. It was the time of day when all three kids often got together to plan some project or just hang out. By now Kate would be finishing homework and ready for action. She was a better bet than Foster, who might get so involved in reading or drawing that he wouldn't bother to come out at all.

Just as Kate finally emerged from the side door, Ben became

aware of a tickling inside his cupped hands. He wanted to look, to see if the creature had woken up and was moving, but the timing was wrong. Just now he had to act as though he were on top of the situation. If he played this right, Kate would beg for a single glance at his treasure.

2

All *Kate could* think of was that in two more days it would be the weekend. Then she would bring home her kitten, Blackberry, from Flint Farm. Never mind that what she had longed for was a puppy. A kitten was better than nothing.

She had done everything her parents asked. That was the bargain: to show them that she was old enough and responsible. Even though it didn't seem fair that she had to do more household stuff than her two older brothers, she hadn't complained. Anyway, the proving time was almost over. Come Saturday, Blackberry would belong to her.

As soon as she caught sight of Ben, she noticed that he was holding something and looking secretive. Ben was good at that. She figured she was supposed to ask what was up. Still, she waited for him to speak first. After all, she never held back with him. Both he and Foster had known about the kitten almost as soon as she had. So let him tell his news.

"Guess what I caught," he finally said to her.

"I can't." Kate could see that whatever was cupped in his hands was small. "Not a kitten," she added.

"Rarer than a kitten," he said. "Much rarer. Guess."

She shook her head. "Just show me."

"Okay," he said, "but you have to come close."

Kate leaned over Ben's hands, which remained closed around the secret inside.

"One guess," he insisted.

Kate drew back. "You said you'd show me." She turned away.

"I will. Don't you want to see?"

But Kate didn't feel like being strung along. She got enough of that from her brothers. "No," she said with finality. "Not anymore."

It took all her strength not to follow him. She knew exactly where he was heading. He would go right past his own house and on to Foster's. She told herself she didn't care if Foster saw the thing first, but she minded all the same. Worse, she minded that she minded. Now she was torn between running to Flint Farm to play with Blackberry and the other kittens and following Ben to Foster's house.

Then it came to her that she could invite Foster to come with his pad and draw pictures of the kittens. These days all he ever drew were shapes, not things. Some of his shape pictures were sort of interesting, but they couldn't come close to what he could make of four playful kittens rolling all over one another on the barn floor.

She took her time so that she wouldn't seem to be following Ben. She even considered stopping to see Miss Ladd, whose house was closer. But that might take too long, especially if Miss Ladd invited her to stay for tea. It would be rude to turn her down.

Instead Kate detoured around behind the Josephsons' in case their dogs were in their outside pen and lonely. But they were indoors today. She could hear them barking in the cellar.

By now Ben was nowhere to be seen. She guessed he was already showing his rare thing to Foster. Kate managed not to run the rest of the way to Foster's house. She managed not to pound on the door either. She just drew a breath, rang the bell once, and waited for Foster to let her in.

3 Foster said, "Give me a hint. What shape is it?"

A few minutes ago Ben might have hinted about a fossil. Now his hatchling dinosaur seemed to be turning somersaults inside his cupped hands. He could barely keep from depositing the thing on the floor.

"It's alive," he said, looking around Foster's kitchen for a safe place to put it. "I don't know if it's dangerous or anything."

Foster got the picture. He opened a cabinet door and hauled out a large mixing bowl. "Does it need water?" he asked.

Ben shrugged. "I found it in the ditch."

Foster hoped it was a baby turtle. It was too early for tree frogs. "Not an insect," he guessed.

Ben nodded. "Not an insect." Then he couldn't stand the tickling anymore and opened his hands over the bowl.

The creature landed on its back. Its underside was gray, but when it flipped itself over, the color was startlingly different, dark and glossy with bright yellow spots.

"A lizard?" asked Foster. "What kind?"

Ben said he had no idea. Together they watched it try to climb out of its smooth-sided prison.

"It wants to escape," Foster said. "You going to let it go?"

"Maybe." Ben hadn't thought that far. First he had to find out what it was and what it did for a living. "It might be rare. It might be worth a lot."

The front doorbell rang. Neither boy made a move to answer it. Foster had just noticed lines like slots going up and down all along the lizard's sides, as if it were marked for slicing. "Where did you say you found it?" he asked Ben.

Kate appeared at the kitchen door, which wasn't locked. She walked in, ignoring Ben and speaking to Foster about the kittens. This was almost his last chance to draw them before they went to their new homes.

Foster said, "Look what Ben found."

Kate glanced into the bowl. The creature was only three or four inches long. Its head wasn't much thicker than its body, which was supported by squat but agile legs that kept trying to hold on to the slippery inside of the bowl. "Put it on the floor," Kate said. "See what it does."

Ben lowered the bowl to the floor and tipped the creature out. It acted dazed, reminding Ben of the way it had first looked. Then it collected itself and took off with surprising speed. "It'll get away," Ben shouted, diving after it.

"There's nowhere to go," Foster told him.

Ben pulled back, still on his knees, while the creature probed at the base of the kitchen door. Then it turned and made its way along the front of the cabinets. Ben relaxed as it distanced itself from the only way out. Only then, before he could react, the creature reached the refrigerator. In an instant it had vanished, beneath or behind or, anyway, out of sight.

4 When *they heard* the car pull into the driveway, they were still lying full length on the floor.

"Quick," Ben ordered, "get rid of all the stuff." He was speaking of the spatula, the flashlight, the roll of newspaper, and the broom, each brought to the refrigerator to aid in the capture of the lizard thing.

Foster drew himself up onto his knees. "Why?"

"We can't let the grown-ups know what's under here," Ben told him.

"Why not?" said Foster. "They'll help."

"It's got to be a secret," Ben said. "Because they might not understand."

The door was opening as Ben scooped up the newspaper and the flashlight and ducked into the living room.

"Hi," said Adele, who wasn't Foster's mother even though she was going to marry his dad. "What's up?"

"Down," Foster told her. "Actually, down and under—"

"Okay, Foster," said Ben, returning empty-handed to the kitchen, "no need to worry about it now." He glared at Kate, who was still lying on her stomach. She got the message. She sat up.

"Worry about what?" asked Foster's dad, following Adele in through the door.

The three children were silent. Ben, who was trying to

enforce the silence, knew that if he didn't supply an answer, Foster or Kate might blurt out the truth. "It's a project," he said. "We can't talk about it yet."

Adele started to pull groceries from a bag. "A school project?" she asked him.

"Not exactly," he answered. "An after-school project. Like homework."

"Good," said Foster's dad. "I'm glad you kids are getting team projects to work on. Foster could use a push in that direction."

Seeing Foster open his mouth to speak, Ben knew he had to separate him from these interested grown-ups. "Actually we were just about to take a break," Ben declared. "We're going to Flint Farm so that Foster can draw kittens." He threw a look at Kate. "Isn't that right?" he demanded.

Rising to her feet, Kate nodded. "The kittens go to their new homes this weekend," she explained to the grown-ups. "It's almost Foster's last chance to see them together."

"Great!" exclaimed Adele. She turned to Foster. "I can't wait to see what you make of real kittens."

Foster sighed. If he didn't go along with Ben and Kate, he would have to face his father's and Adele's growing concern. They wanted him to be more like other kids. If he had to paint and draw instead of joining group activities, the least he could do was produce pictures that ordinary people could recognize.

He dropped the spatula in the sink and leaned the broom against the wall. No sign remained of the efforts to locate the lizard. Sticking his hands in his pockets, he followed Ben and Kate out through the living room.

"What about your sketchbook?" Adele called after him.

"Foster," Ben whispered, "look real."

After Foster left to get his drawing pad, Kate told Ben to leave Foster alone. It wasn't Foster's fault that the thing was lost under his refrigerator.

"It's not lost," Ben retorted. "We know where it is. We just can't get at it with the whole world standing around watching."

Each thinking private thoughts, the three set off for Flint Farm.

5 *The kittens were* asleep in a patch of sunlight. They had made a nest inside a coiled rope they must have been playing with. The end of the rope was frayed, and a few fibers from it still clung to some of the tiny claws.

Kate wanted to be the first to wake the kittens, but not until she could figure out which was hers. Four black kittens with only a little white here and there were hard to tell apart. It was important to show that she and Blackberry already knew each other.

As far as Ben was concerned, this visit was simply a cooling-off period for Foster, who couldn't appreciate what was at stake. Ben would have to count on him to give an all clear just as soon the grown-ups were out of the way.

Foster stared at the kittens and the rope. He saw circles within circles, separate yet connected. He saw curves and spirals and, above them, dust motes whirling in a sunbeam.

Kate squatted and stroked one furry head after another. A

black ear flicked off her touch. A paw stretched out, toes and claws extended, before curling back in sleep. How could she ever sort them out? If she picked up the wrong kitten, Ben would never let her forget it.

"Maybe we should leave them alone," she whispered. "To give Foster time to draw them," she added.

But Foster wasn't drawing. He just gazed at the coiled heap.

Ben figured that Foster was annoyed at him. So he tried to explain where he was coming from. "The thing is, grown-ups take over. Especially where it's something rare and valuable and maybe endangered."

"Your lizard thing is endangered right now," Kate pointed out. "It could starve in Foster's kitchen. It could die there."

"Right," said Ben. "So we have to make a plan." He nudged Foster. "You have to be a part of the plan since you live there."

Foster pulled himself out of the circles he was looking at. "Okay," he said. "Dad can move the refrigerator."

"No," Kate told him. "It might run over the lizard."

"No," Ben shouted, waking the kittens. "Don't you get it? Your father might not let me keep it."

Foster didn't get it. Why should his father care what Ben kept? Even though his dad never actually said so, Foster could tell that he thought Ben was a typical kid who did normal things. A boy with a lizard was a lot less worrisome than a boy who drew pictures that needed to be explained.

One kitten detached itself from the others and stretched. Not hers, Kate saw, not Blackberry. Another kitten rose, arched its back, and jumped over the rope. Kate was almost certain it was Blackberry.

"First off," Ben declared, "we have to plan."

All the kittens scampered outside. Kate followed them.

"Are we in this together or what?" Ben demanded, his voice rising again.

Kate was out of earshot. Foster was staring at the rope, fixing what he had seen in his mind's eye. Those two were hopeless. Neither seemed to understand that Ben had found an extraordinary animal, maybe one in a million, and it needed to be rescued.

Kate reappeared, her kitten in her arms. "Blackberry!" she announced in triumph. The day after tomorrow she would take him home.

If she weren't so hung up on this kitten, thought Ben, she would be able to give some thought to the lizard thing. Somehow he had to figure out how to keep the creature happy so that it stayed hidden under the refrigerator until Foster's dad and Adele went to work tomorrow. Then he had to figure out how to retrieve it before they came home again.

He drew a deep breath and said, "We ought to make what we said about its being an after-school project true." Maybe this approach would appeal to Foster, who was hooked on being honest. "A team project, like Foster's father said."

"That was your idea," Kate told him, rubbing her chin on Blackberry's soft fur.

"In a team," Ben continued, "with everyone working together." He paused, giving them a chance to agree. "If we keep this to ourselves," he went on, "then we'll all end up like maybe being famous. We'll get our pictures in the paper."

"Why?" asked Foster.

"Because we'll have this, like, rare lizard thing that is an amazing find. Maybe everyone thought it was extinct. Maybe no one knows that any of this kind of lizard still exists."

"What kind of lizard is it?" asked Foster.

"We don't know yet. We can't find out till we have it again and can study it carefully and then, like, look it up. Foster, you draw it, and then we'll compare it with pictures in a book about lizards."

"Why not take a picture of it?" said Kate.

"Because whoever develops the film might leak out the news to the press. We need to keep it secret. And if it's an unknown kind of lizard, then we can name it."

"You can't call it Blackberry," Kate said.

"Not that kind of name," Ben told her. "A scientific name that mentions our team and where it was found."

"Are you saying it's our lizard," Kate asked him, "not just yours?"

Ben swallowed. "Ours," he finally answered. That was one hard word for him to speak.

6 The entire walk back to Foster's house was spent figuring out a lizard menu. "Cheerios, for sure," said Ben, whose little sister, Daisy, ate almost nothing else. "I can bring over a handful."

"What if they're bad for it?" asked Kate. "They might have some fatal ingredient."

"You could try our granola," Foster said. "It's homemade and natural."

"Okay then, you throw some under the fridge. But don't let anyone see you." Ben was still worried about Foster, who was always in danger of being truthful.

Kate said, "I'll do lettuce. What about meat?"

They were stumped. Ben guessed it would have to be raw. He hoped it didn't have to be alive as well. "The trouble is we don't know what lizards eat."

"In nature movies they catch insects," Foster said.

Ben nodded. He remembered that, too.

"We're not even absolutely sure that it is a lizard," Kate pointed out. "So far it's just a lizard thing."

"Yes, a liz-thing. That can be our code word," Ben said. "Liz-thing. No one would ever guess what we're talking about, not even a scientist."

Kate left the boys and ran into her house to look for ants, flies, or moths. First she tried the kitchen. It was too clean for bugs. Next she tried the houseplants. Where were those white flies Mom always fussed about? Giving up for now, she stopped to grab a lettuce leaf and ran back to the boys.

"We need a dirtier place," she told them. "Ben's house."

But there were two problems there. One was Ben's mother; the other was his sister.

Sometimes Kate wished her mom stayed home like Ben's mom, who was really nice, but Daisy was part of the mom package. Probably not worth it. This afternoon they both made the insect hunt impossible.

"Did you lose something?" Mrs. Addario asked in her nice way. "Can I help?"

"Me, too!" Daisy exclaimed. "Help."

"You'll step on it," Ben told her as he ran his hand under the baseboard radiator.

Farther along the wall Foster fetched out a dust ball filled with pieces of toys and paper clips.

"What will she step on?" Ben's mother asked. "I mean," she continued, glancing at Foster's haul, "most things are already broken."

Kate clapped and shouted from the kitchen, "Got it!"

As she opened her clasped hands, everyone crowded around to see what she had.

"A meal moth?" Ben's mother sounded puzzled. "You're looking for meal moths?"

"Insects," Foster said. "Actually—"

Before he could go on, Ben said, "It's a project for after school."

"Only it shouldn't be dead," Foster finished.

"Dead is all right," said Mrs. Addario. "Where meal moths are concerned," she added. "If you ask me."

Ben touched the flattened meal moth. "I guess it's better than nothing," he remarked.

Daisy reached up toward Kate's hand.

"Mom," Ben wailed, "she'll smush it."

"It's already smushed," Mrs. Addario responded. "Let her see it. I'll get a magnifying glass."

"Give it to me," Ben told Kate, holding out a hand over Daisy's head. In an instant the meal moth had disappeared into his pocket. "All gone," he told his little sister, who burst into tears. Ben snatched the dust ball from Foster and presented Daisy with the arm of an action figure and a paper clip.

"What now?" Mrs. Addario demanded, returning without the magnifying glass. "What did you do?" she said to Ben.

"Nothing," he answered. "I didn't do anything to her." He appealed to Kate and Ben. "Did I?"

"Nothing," they assured Mrs. Addario.

She took away the action arm and the clip because Daisy could choke on them. Daisy cried harder.

"That's the trouble with toddlers," Ben declared. "They're too dumb to know you're saving their life."

His mother threw him a look before carrying Daisy into the living room.

"Let's go," Ben said, his voice low. "It's hopeless here."

So they took off. At least they had something to work with now: a handful of Daisy's Cheerios, a dead meal moth, and a lettuce leaf.

Of course they still had to deal with Foster's father and Adele. That could be tricky since those two were into sharing in a big way. Foster would have to keep them busy long enough for Ben and Kate to shove the morsels of food out of their sight yet temptingly close to the liz-thing.

7 By *the time* Foster had waited out the grown-ups in the kitchen and was able to let Kate and Ben inside, he was ready to give the liz-thing back to Ben. Tricking grown-ups was too nerve racking. It wasn't so much that he was afraid of being caught with his hand in the granola jar. It was all that phony talk about the after-school project. It led to impossible questions. Without Ben right beside him to make up answers on the spot, Foster just clammed up.

Good smells wafted around the kitchen. The grown-ups sipping wine in the living room would be back soon to dish up supper.

Silently Ben and Kate dropped to their knees in front of the refrigerator.

"Any sign of it?" Ben whispered to Foster. "Where's the flashlight?"

Foster opened a drawer as quietly as possible and pulled out a flashlight.

"No time to hunt," Kate murmured. "Let's just leave the food and look tomorrow." But when she tried to shove the lettuce underneath, it wouldn't roll or slide like the Cheerios. Standing up, she caught sight of a wooden spoon beside the stove. She used that to push the lettuce leaf farther in. "Moth," she whispered to Ben.

Reaching into his pocket, he realized he was probably lying on the meal moth. He decided not to mention this. Instead he deposited what remained of it a few inches from where the lettuce had gone. Then he blew as hard as he could to send the tiny moth tumbling out of sight. He guessed there must be another wing in his pocket. But the grown-ups were stirring. Time to leave the kitchen to Foster and his family.

Ben and Kate quietly retreated. Only Ben had an idea. He called to Foster in the softest voice he could manage, "We can come back in the middle of the night when your folks are sleeping."

Stepping outside to answer him, Foster shut the door. "You mean, really late?"

"I can bring another flashlight. So can Kate."

"I'm not allowed out after dark," Kate said.

"Of course," Ben said to her. "No one is. That's why we have to do it secretly when everyone else is in bed."

Kate shook her head. "I've spent three whole weeks being good, and I'm not about to break any rules before this weekend."

"Not even if it's a matter of life and death?"

"It isn't," she declared firmly. "That liz-thing has plenty to eat. Unless it's super fussy, it can't starve overnight."

Ben turned his back on her. "How about it?" he asked Foster. "A deal?"

Foster glanced at the door. Why had he even come outside to hear this? "I wouldn't wake up," he said. "Nothing wakes me."

"That doesn't matter," Ben told him. "Stay awake." Seeing that he wasn't winning over either of them, he turned on his heel. "Okay," he said, "forget it. I guess you guys don't care as much as I do. Because I'm the one that found it. I discovered what could be a really rare and marvelous—"

"Foster?" Adele was opening the kitchen door and calling him to supper. "What are you doing out there?" she asked as Kate scooted after Ben.

"Stuff," said Foster with relief. "Just stuff." He almost told her he was saying good-night to Ben and Kate. Only Ben didn't want the grown-ups to know they were there. Foster couldn't imagine why it mattered except that Ben liked to make things risky and complicated.

"Hungry?" Adele asked Foster as she held the door for him.

Foster nodded but couldn't help blurting, "I took a handful

of granola a while ago." He could see how dangerous it was to speak. He might end up telling too much.

In the kitchen his dad ladled out lasagna. Foster couldn't wait to dig in.

8 *The next afternoon,* when the school bus dropped them off at the end of Flint Farm Road, the three kids headed straight for Foster's house. Ben walked faster and faster and then started to run. It was important for him to be the first one there. Only when he reached the door did he remember that Foster had the key.

"Hurry up, you guys," he shouted.

Kate and Foster were talking about using the vacuum cleaner to get the liz-thing.

"There's a special tool for window blinds that's small and flat," Kate said.

"We don't have window blinds," Foster told her. "We might not have that tool. Anyway, if it sucks even part of the lizard in, it could hurt it."

"We'll take everything out of the refrigerator to make it lighter," Ben said as Foster unlocked the door and let them in. "Then we can move it."

Kate didn't think it was the food inside that made the refrigerator so heavy, but she didn't want to start an argument. "First we have to see where it is," she pointed out, rummaging in her backpack for her flashlight.

It wasn't until all three flashlights were crisscrossing the darkness that Ben was able to see anything at all. "I think that's the lettuce," he said. He tried to look from another angle, but nothing showed up.

Kate took a turn. "Cheerios," she declared. And then she shouted, "Yes!" She drew back. "It's there. It's moving."

"Let me see," Ben said, sliding down and lying as flat as he could.

"It's Foster's turn," Kate reminded him.

Ben couldn't see the liz-thing at all. "Are you sure you didn't imagine it?" he asked Kate.

She wasn't sure, but she refused to say so. If Ben took over again, she wasn't going to help anymore.

Foster left his flashlight in place and went to look for something less powerful than the vacuum cleaner. He returned with a dust mop. "Where is it?" he asked Kate. "I have to get the mop in behind it."

"Sort of the middle," she told him. "Unless it moved."

"You look and tell me," he said.

"I should do that," Ben said. "My arms are longer than Foster's."

"You're doing the light," Kate told him firmly.

Ben couldn't believe how she was taking over. "You're not the boss," he said.

"No one is," she retorted.

Thinking that he should never have made them joint owners of his rare, valuable, and soon-to-be-recovered lizard, he shifted the flashlight to make the beam shine back and forth under the refrigerator.

"No, no," Kate was telling Foster. "I can't see anything now. Can you keep that mop back on your side? That's right. Way over."

Foster grunted. "That's as far as it'll go."

"Okay." The lizard was retreating from the mop. Or was it the light that bothered it? "Now bring the mop forward. Very slowly."

Foster followed her directions as she guided the mop head behind the lizard.

"It's coming," Kate announced. "Are you ready, Ben?"

He was. Leaving the flashlight on, he slithered close to Kate.

As the mop began to emerge, he was afraid it had somehow missed or lost the lizard. But then he saw the tail. The lizard was entangled in the mop's soft fibers. Was it all right?

Without a word the three of them set to work. Each strand of the mop had to be freed, one at a time. The lizard didn't seem frightened. Ben worried that it was too quiet. Maybe it was dying.

"There!" he exclaimed when the last strand was unwound from the lizard's body. He scooped it into his hand.

Six eyes stared down at the creature, and its two eyes, huge in the blunt-nosed head, seemed to stare back.

"We should give it a chance to rest," Kate said.

"It is resting," Ben pointed out.

"It needs a place of its own," Kate told him. "In case we scare it."

"Do you have a box?" Ben asked Foster.

What Foster could quickly provide was the glass mixing bowl. "Wait," he told Ben, and he went outside to scrape some dirt and leaf mold from the edge of the driveway. "There!" he said. "See if it likes that."

As soon as Ben set the lizard on the dirt in the bowl, it tried to climb out again. It still couldn't because the bowl was too slippery. "We'll have to find something better to keep it in," Ben said.

"Maybe it's just hungry," Kate suggested. "Or thirsty. Is there a really little dish we could put in there for water?"

Foster hunted around until he found the top of a glass jar. It held about half an inch of water, even though some spilled as he set it inside the bowl. The lizard seemed to sense the nearness of water. It scurried up to the jar top, swayed briefly, and climbed right in.

The kids grinned at one another. They had got something right. Now all they had to do was figure out where to keep this creature and what else to feed it. To do that, first they had to find out exactly what sort of lizard thing it was.

9 No, Ben decided, first he had to get it out of Foster's house. First take it home.

Kate went along with him because his house was on the way to hers. But she left him at his driveway and hurried on. This whole lizard business had robbed her and Blackberry of important bonding time. Mrs. Flint had told Kate that advance bonding would help the kitten settle into his new home.

By the time Kate reached the barn she was breathless. Where

were the kittens? She ran between the rows of old cow stanchions to the far door. There she had to stop because of mud. Turning back, she tried the milking parlor. After that she climbed up to the hayloft. Mr. Flint didn't allow children up there because they messed up hay or else they might fall through the hatch and blame him. But she had to find Blackberry.

And there they were, all four kittens, skittering and pouncing at light patterns on the nearly bare floor. One kitten climbed onto stacked bales of hay. It crouched, stared at the others, and then hurled itself down. By the time the kitten landed, its littermates were well out of range.

Kate waited awhile, watching but staying out of the way. When a pigeon flew in, the kittens' play came to an abrupt halt. In an instant all four of them froze. Then they took cover. Wondering why they were afraid of a pigeon, Kate hurried over to Blackberry. With her back against the hay bales, her knees propped to turn her lap into a sort of nest, she held Blackberry quietly. He yawned and closed his eyes.

She was still sitting there, dreamy and blissful, when Ben's shout shattered the peace.

"Kate? Where are you?" he called at the top of his lungs.

Kate heard Mrs. Flint speak to him about the racket he was making.

"Well, where is she?" he demanded. "How can she hear me if I keep my voice down?"

Mrs. Flint spoke again. "Try looking."

Guessing that Mrs. Flint was returning to the house, Kate waited a moment before rising. Then she carried the sleeping kitten to the upper loading door and called softly to Ben.

"You're not allowed up there," he told her. "I need to talk to you."

Without answering, she lowered Blackberry into the heap of his littermates. Then she went down the stairs.

Ben was waiting for her. "What were you doing up there? I've been looking all over for you." He didn't wait for a reply. "We've got problems," he told her. "Big time."

Kate didn't think she had problems, big or little. After her quiet rest with Blackberry she felt wonderful.

"It's Daisy," Ben went on. "She won't leave our liz-thing alone."

Kate said, "So tell your mother."

"She's on Daisy's side. She always is."

"So what do you want me to do?" Kate asked him.

"Keep it. For now. It'll be safe in your room."

"But I'm getting Blackberry," Kate told him.

"Right, and didn't your mom make you promise to keep him shut in your room when you're not with him?"

Kate nodded.

"So the liz-thing'll be safe, at least for a while. That'll give us time to figure out what to do with it. That's why it has to go to your house. Do you see?"

Kate didn't see exactly. She wanted to devote her time to Blackberry. "What do I have to do?" she asked.

"Nothing," Ben said excitedly. "Nothing at all. We'll get food for it as soon as we find out what kind of food it likes. Maybe you could keep its water full. That's all."

"I have to tell my mom, though," Kate said.

Ben nodded. "Mine knows now, too. But she doesn't understand that it's probably rare and valuable."

Kate heaved a sigh. Ben sounded desperate. How could she refuse to keep the liz-thing for the time being when she was getting nearly her heart's desire this very weekend?

10 *In school on* Friday Ben, Kate, and Foster set out to identify the liz-thing. Books in the school library didn't show them what they were looking for, though.

Kate gave up as soon as she discovered that there were more than 3,000 kinds of lizards. The kind curled in the jar top in the mixing bowl on her bureau looked a little like one picture and nothing at all like any of the other seven photographs she saw. She would never have time to look for pictures of the other 2,093. Starting tomorrow, her new kitten would need her undivided attention.

Ben was discouraged, too. Then he came across a *National Geographic* magazine picture of a fossil dinosaur embryo in its egg. That embryo looked almost exactly like his liz-thing. Everything he had imagined about it seemed to be coming true. But when he asked the science teacher whether something frozen in ice for thousands of years could thaw out and be alive, she shook her head. "Only in movies," she told him.

"But some things happen for the first time," Ben insisted. "So couldn't this?"

"Couldn't what?" asked the teacher.

Ben wasn't ready to share his rare, valuable, first-of-its-kind, sensational find with any grown-up, not even his favorite teacher. First he had to get all his facts straight.

Meanwhile Foster went on reading. He did this partly because he liked to read and partly because his reading led to a description of a giant lizard called a Komodo dragon. That made him think about all the dragon pictures he had ever seen. Since it was obvious that the liz-thing in the glass mixing bowl was nothing like a real four-hundred-pound, man-eating lizard or, for that matter, like any fire-breathing story dragon, he forgot that he was supposed to be identifying the liz-thing. Instead he began to draw dragons. Tomorrow at his art lesson he would start right off with imaginary beasts.

When the three kids met during recess after lunch, Foster listened to Ben's dinosaur-embryo theory, but his mind was still on dragons. Now it occurred to him that most dragons had wings. "Pterodactyls flew," he said. "Dinosaurs might be the ancestors of birds."

"I know that," Ben said impatiently. "Everyone knows that."

"Maybe dragons are the ancestors of dinosaurs," Foster concluded. "Or the other way around."

"We're talking about a real live lizard," Ben said, his voice rising.

He turned to Kate. "What did you find out?"

Kate told him she hadn't learned anything useful.

"So you'd better agree with me then," he declared. "If our liz-thing is a dinosaur embryo, we have a mystery to solve. No one's ever known a fossil to come back to life except in movies."

"Can embryos live outside eggs?" she asked.

"I don't know," Ben nearly shouted. "If I had more help, maybe we could find out."

Several kids glanced his way, and he lowered his voice. "This is a lead we have to follow. Okay?"

"How do we do that?" Kate asked him.

Ben was stumped. "I guess . . . ," he said, mulling over this question, "I guess we might have to start asking grown-ups. But don't give anything away," he added. "It's got to be kept secret until we can make an announcement."

Kate figured she could go next door to see Miss Ladd this afternoon and ask her. She doubted that Miss Ladd knew much about lizards or embryos, but at least Kate would be doing her part. Then she could devote all of Saturday to Blackberry.

Foster always looked forward to Saturday and his art lesson with Mr. Torpor, who lived past Kate's house and was the closest person to Flint Farm. He repaired bicycles and walked around the countryside and painted pictures of everything he noticed. He wasn't much of a talker, but maybe if Foster drew the liz-thing, Mr. Torpor could shed some light on it.

But already Foster's thoughts were veering away from Ben's mystery. He recalled the ring of kittens and how they made circles within circles inside the coiled rope so that you could hardly tell which paw or tail belonged to which body. They were a little bit like the liz-thing curled inside the round jar cover. If there was a link between the liz-thing and a dinosaur or a dragon, would they fit together in some kind of circle, too?

11

As *soon as* Ben walked through his front door, he asked if he could use the computer.

His mother said, "No games before homework."

"It *is* homework," Ben told her. "That project."

"Okay, then," she said, "as soon as Grandma calls back. I have to leave the phone free until she does."

Ben waited a few minutes. The telephone didn't ring. He found his mother in Daisy's room assembling some baby gadget. Things were strewn all over the floor.

"Why don't you call Grandma?" he asked.

"Not home," Mom mumbled, her lips pressed together, holding screws.

Daisy picked up the screwdriver. Mom sounded an alarm without words. Ben took the tool away from Daisy, who promptly sat down to cry.

"Stracter," Mom ordered.

"Stricter?" Ben asked. It was high time for more strictness with his little sister. But that didn't seem to be what Mom was saying. Stroke her? Ben wondered. He wasn't about to do that. Subtract her? That was more like it. He'd been prepared to subtract Daisy from certain parts of the house ever since she took to climbing everything in and out of sight.

Mom spit the screws into her hands and said, "For goodness' sake, Ben, distract her."

"Oh," he said, reaching for Daisy. "Let's go swing."

Instantly she quieted. She loved having him stand on the

swing with his legs on either side of her. He could make the swing go really high that way.

"Acket," Mom said, the screws between her lips again.

Daisy wasn't making a racket anymore, so that couldn't be what Mom was telling him.

"Jacket," Daisy said, clear as day. She grabbed his hand and pulled him to the stairs.

"Oots," Mom called after them.

"Boots, okay," he shouted back to her.

On the swing with Daisy chortling and then shrieking with delight, Ben almost forgot that she was a pest. But later, when he was searching on the computer for dinosaur embryos and swamped with information he couldn't use, she began to get on his nerves again.

"Mom," he called, "take Daisy."

His mother appeared. "What's this about?" she asked, glancing at the screen.

"Can't I have some privacy?" Ben wailed.

His mother said, "What are you looking for?"

"Fossils," he answered. "Dinosaur eggs." He turned in his chair and faced her. "Could an embryo live outside its egg?"

Mom shook her head. "I don't think so. I don't really know. I mean, there might be really primitive . . ." Her voice trailed off.

Pretty soon she was sitting beside him, Daisy in her lap, watching the screen. "Maybe," she concluded, "an embryo in its final phase. Like a tadpole, which is still almost an embryo when it's swimming around before its limbs are fully grown."

Ben grinned at her. "Cool!" he exclaimed. That was a good enough answer. Now he felt ready to look for some possible connection between his liz-thing and an ancient dinosaur. "Thanks," he said. Then he added, "I'm all set now. I'll be fine."

His mother smiled, shrugged, and took Daisy away with her. Left to himself, Ben set to work in earnest.

12

Kate thought Friday would never end. Her mother had told her to get her room kittenproof, which meant putting away anything breakable. But that didn't take long. Neither did finding the right corner for Blackberry's special cushion or putting his litter box between the chair and the bookshelf. As the afternoon dragged on, Kate rearranged the cushion and the box, and then changed her mind again and put them back where they had begun.

Finally she went outside. On her way to Flint Farm she passed the place where Ben said he had found the liz-thing. Only then did she remember that she was supposed to be finding out anything she could about eggs and stuff in case it was a baby dinosaur somehow come to life.

She slowed to inspect the deep ditch that started along the side of the road below Mr. Torpor's house. If the liz-thing were a dinosaur baby or embryo, wouldn't there be bits of eggshell around? As far as she could tell, as she walked slowly enough to peer into it, there was nothing that looked the least like an egg or a part of an egg. But it occurred to her that here, where water collected and the soil and fill were loose, she might find more insects for the lizard.

She knelt and stirred some of the rubble. It was icy cold. When she heard a car, she scrambled to her feet and stepped way back. After the car had sped by, she noticed a few roadside weeds in the ditch, not the brittle ones from last year but new green sprouts, early for the season. She pulled up a few with their roots still embedded in gravelly soil.

Then, of course, she had to turn back instead of going on to see Blackberry. Well, she would be bringing him home first thing tomorrow. The least she could do now was make a more natural place for the liz-thing.

She made two more trips outside to dig up moss that might live for a few days in the glass bowl. She even planted an acorn with a stem growing out of it like a tiny tree, and she brought in a whole earthworm in case the liz-thing ate that sort of thing.

As soon as the liz-thing garden was finished, she swept off what had spilled onto her bureau, checked the floor, and pulled her bedside rug over the worst of the outdoor dirt. She still hadn't made any headway on dinosaur embryos and eggs.

When she presented herself at Miss Ladd's front door, Miss Ladd said, "I don't suppose it's too late for tea. Do you?"

Kate loved teatime with Miss Ladd. There were always thin ginger biscuits on a blue-and-white plate and milk and honey for the smoky tea. And they sat in the parlor on brown velvet chairs with rounded backs.

But when Miss Ladd asked Kate what she had been up to, Kate didn't know what to say. Since the liz-thing was supposed to be a secret, she talked about Blackberry, who was coming tomorrow for good, forever.

Miss Ladd sipped her tea.

"Did you ever have a cat or a dog?" Kate asked.

Miss Ladd shook her head. "When I was a dancer, I traveled too much to keep a pet. It wouldn't have been fair to an animal. By the time I retired here, I was used to not having one. Instead I took to gardening. Flowers are my family."

Kate wondered whether Miss Ladd was ever lonely. She always seemed so pleased when Kate came to see her. "What about birds?" Kate asked, hoping that this subject might lead to eggs and embryos.

"What about birds?" Miss Ladd asked. "I feed some over the winter."

Kate scowled. It was hard to talk about something you weren't supposed to mention, especially with such a good friend. "Any nests?" she asked feebly. "Do you ever see baby birds and eggs and stuff?"

Miss Ladd nodded. "You know I do. I've shown you greedy birds like sparrows feeding greedier babies, and I've shown you shy ones like phoebes. Why?"

Kate shook her head. "I was just wondering. About eggs," she added lamely.

Miss Ladd sent her a puzzled look. Then she said, "You'll have to watch your kitten during nesting and fledging season. You don't want him going after baby birds."

"He won't. I'll train him not to. Besides, Blackberry's going to be really good."

"It's in the nature of the beast," said Miss Ladd. "Even in a good kitten, which I'm sure yours is."

Kate bit into her third ginger biscuit. Somehow the talk had shifted from the subject she had come to discuss. If Miss Ladd, who had never even owned a cat, knew more about kittens than eggs, she couldn't provide much of an answer to Kate's muddled question.

So she relaxed. As she finished her tea, the afternoon sun cast long, bent shadows from behind bare trees. The fretted light softened the colors in Miss Ladd's parlor and darkened the bleached tones still visible through the window. Even after the swish-swish of passing cars broke the stillness and became a steady drone, the parlor seemed like a place apart.

Kate stayed until Miss Ladd gently sent her home.

13 On *Saturday morning* Foster met Kate just as she headed out to Flint Farm. "You can come over later," she told him. "After Blackberry settles in. You want to draw or paint him? A really good picture would make a great present. Most people like kittens better than shapes."

Foster nodded. He didn't tell her that he was drawing dragons now.

"So are you coming?" she asked when he stopped in front of Mr. Torpor's house.

"It's my art lesson," he said.

"Oh." No one seemed to realize what this day meant to Kate. At least Mom and Dad had offered to drive her to make sure the kitten wouldn't escape on the road. But Kate had proudly insisted that she could carry Blackberry all the way.

There was a note on Mr. Torpor's door telling Foster to go in and get started. Mr. Torpor never said where he went when he wasn't home. Once he had told Foster that the cycle of life dictated his schedule. That was a kind of joke because he repaired bicycles for a living. But Foster knew that Mr. Torpor meant the cycle of life in the fields and woods. People put up with his ways because he could fix most things better than anyone else.

What he did best of all, though, was to draw and paint. At least that's what Foster thought. He helped himself to a large sheet of paper and spread it out on the living-room floor.

Often he used the easel beside the table, first drawing with a soft pencil or charcoal. But today he couldn't wait to get his hands on a paintbrush. There was no other furniture in the room, no carpet to worry about. Mr. Torpor didn't bother to clean up drips and brushstrokes that missed the paper. He believed that sooner or later, as the floor became crisscrossed with the outline of many sheets of paper, it would become an accidental work of art.

By the time Mr. Torpor returned from wherever he had been, Foster had painted two pictures, one of a single dragon biting its own tail, the other of a circle of dragons. Mr. Torpor loomed above him, studying the two paintings. Foster, crouched on the floor, looked at Mr. Torpor's muddy boots.

"Odd," Mr. Torpor commented. He pointed to the single dragon. "This one looks like a cross between a salamander and a cat."

"It doesn't have wings," said Foster.

"True," Mr. Torpor agreed. Then he added, "Did you think it ought to?"

Foster shrugged. "It's just that dragons usually do. Like those." He nodded at the circle of dragons.

"But that's what's good about dragons," Mr. Torpor told him. "They can be whatever you decide since they're not real."

"Well, then, like pterodactyls." Foster swiveled around so that he was looking up at the tall man beside him. "Where do dragons come from?" he asked.

"Ah," said Mr. Torpor, "good question. You mean, from the human imagination or from some natural model?"

Foster thought of the Komodo dragon, which was, after all, a giant lizard that had been given a dragon name. "Yes. Maybe the first dragon was a winged lizard, or maybe it was a dinosaur."

"Maybe. But not being certain has its advantage. We can combine our knowledge with what we choose to design. There's no right or wrong dragon, wings or no wings."

Suddenly a new idea rushed into Foster's head. Peeling off another sheet of paper, he started all over again, this time with charcoal. Swiftly he drew a huge circle. At first he was nearly lying across the paper. Then he reared back and rose on his knees. Upon the circle he drew one creature and then another, each different but connected.

"Ah," declared Mr. Torpor as the outlined circle was transformed into a ring of beasts. There was a sort of tadpole, something else like a tiny dinosaur, a creature like the enormous lizard with the dragon name, and finally a soaring beast with webbed talons, ruffled wings, and fire breath.

Mr. Torpor nodded. "The Great Chain of Being," he murmured.

Foster didn't ask what that meant. He sat back on his heels, not yet ready for paint. He needed to look and think awhile. He needed to ponder the origin of dragons. He needed to draw

another circle, this time not round, but egg shaped. He needed to place inside it a first creature, a thing that would become.

14

Ben *spent most* of Saturday morning hounding his parents with questions they couldn't answer. He wanted to know how you could announce a scientific discovery so that no one else stole the credit. He wanted to know how someone who wasn't grown up could present his discovery so that people took it seriously.

"You'll have to be more specific," said his father, who was in the backyard making a brush pile from branches that had fallen during the winter's ice storms.

Ben pried up a cluster of acorns stuck to withered oak leaves and tossed it on the brush pile. To get his mother and father to think about what he was asking meant that he had to work along with them.

"Scientific discoveries have to be verified," his father told him.

"What's 'verified'?" Ben asked.

His father paused to scrape rubble clinging to the rake. "The discovery has to be found true by people who know a lot about the subject and have nothing to gain from supporting the findings. Ben, it's usually a complicated process that takes a long time. How long depends on what kind of discovery you're talking about."

"Can you two watch Daisy?" Ben's mother called from the driveway.

Ben groaned. Daisy in tow meant the end of serious conversation. "Where are you going?" he asked his mother. Maybe he could go with her and press on with his questions in the car.

But she said she had an appointment and would be back in an hour or so. Now Ben was trapped. He couldn't exactly walk away from his father just because of Daisy, but with her around he wasn't likely to get his dad to pay close enough attention to the pressing questions.

For the next hour he and his father continued to clean up the yard while Daisy helped herself to sticks from the brush pile and left them to be gathered all over again.

By the time she was growing bored and cranky, both Ben and his dad were ready to quit. They all went inside for a snack.

While his dad shook Cheerios into a plastic bowl for Daisy, Ben looked around the kitchen with a critical eye. The press might want to take pictures in here, since this was like the place where the dinosaur embryo had nearly been lost.

Where would a television camera set up to film the scene? Would they want a reenactment? That might be going too far. Could you expose a rare, valuable, one-of-its-kind, previously-thought-extinct creature to so much fuss? Ben doubted it. He would have to act out the tense drama without putting the liz-thing at risk. Also, it would probably be best not to clutter the limited space in front of the refrigerator with too many kids. One would be enough.

Sometime this afternoon or tomorrow he would call a meeting with Kate and Foster. Even if they turned up with useful information, it was clear that there was a long way to go before the existence of a live dinosaur embryo could be revealed to the outside world. So this wasn't the time to claim the spotlight for himself and make the other kids mad. Right now they needed to stick together, to share in their splendid discovery.

Well, actually, it was still Ben's discovery. He was the one who had found and captured it. Only that wasn't the point, at least not for now.

It wasn't getting any easier for Ben to keep in mind that the liz-thing belonged to them all.

15 *Blackberry must have* just woken up from a nap because he was so wired he nearly managed to squirm out of Kate's arms. Mrs. Flint came to the rescue. Since she had to drive to town anyway, she would drop off Kate and her kitten on the way.

Kate didn't have to prove to Mrs. Flint that she was able to handle her own kitten. All these weeks Mrs. Flint had been teaching her how to pick up and hold the kittens and when to leave them alone. So Kate gratefully climbed into Mrs. Flint's car for the short ride home.

But once Blackberry was inside Kate's house, things got out of hand.

"He doesn't know about furniture," said Kate, already having to defend the kitten as he scrambled onto the back of the sofa and began to claw the upholstery.

"Don't pull him," Kate's mother ordered. "First detach the claws."

Tears sprang into Kate's eyes. "Detach his claws?"

"From the furniture," her father explained.

"Wild!" commented one of Kate's brothers, glancing into the living room. "Don't let it near my stuff."

By now Kate had Blackberry in her grasp again. "He's never done anything like this before," she said. But how could she be sure? Probably he clawed things like hay bales that didn't matter.

"Why don't you let him get used to your room first?" her father suggested. "Then later, when he's calmed down, you can introduce him to the rest of the house."

Kate passed her other brother on the stairs. He reached over to pat Blackberry, who batted him with one free forepaw. Her brother laughed and went on down the stairs.

As soon as she had the door closed, Kate let Blackberry jump to the floor. He ran all over her room, his back arched, his tail all fuzzed out. First he pretended to be alarmed by her slippers; then he attacked one, rolling over and over with it.

Kate stayed with him until he began to slow down. When he mewed pitifully, she couldn't tell whether he was missing the other kittens or was hungry. She slipped out the door and went downstairs to get some milk. Even though Mrs. Flint had said that he wouldn't need milk anymore, Kate thought it might comfort him to have some.

While he lapped from his new dish, she went to join her family. She guessed from their lowered voices that they were discussing her kitten. She would stand up for Blackberry if anyone was saying mean things about him.

But as soon as she entered the dining room, the talk broke off. Pretending not to notice, she helped herself to a slice of cold toast. She had been too excited to eat this morning and had skipped breakfast.

"We'll give this kitten time and his own space," Dad said to her. "Right?" He looked at the rest of the family.

Everyone nodded. "It's a time of adjustment," Mom remarked. "Just remember that you have to set limits from the start so that we can all live together without . . ." She didn't finish. Then she added, "In the beginning he'll need watching and training."

"I know," Kate answered. If she failed to civilize this kitten, she wouldn't be allowed to keep him. "Like Dad said," she continued, "we'll start with my room."

Just then something crashed overhead. Kate leaped up from her chair, aware of all eyes on her. She raced back up to her room to find Blackberry tugging the lamp cord. The lamp lay on the floor in one piece, only the bulb broken. But in the few minutes she had been downstairs the kitten had managed to knock other things from their places. Kate's hairbrush poked out from beneath her bed. The trinket box her grandmother had given her was tipped over. It looked to Kate as though Blackberry had cruised all about the room, landing on every possible surface, including the top of the bureau, the window-sill, and the bookcase.

On her way to get the dustpan and broom, she reported to her parents that everything was under control. She was in such a hurry to get back upstairs that she forgot to bring a new bulb. By the time she had swept up all the broken glass, Blackberry was stretching and yawning. She carried him to her bed and stayed with him until he grew drowsy. Curled against her pillow, he was the picture of innocence.

While he slept, she put her room in order, hiding most movable objects, even if they weren't breakable. It was while she was restoring order that she glanced into the glass mixing bowl and saw her tiny tree toppled, the moss furrowed, the jar cover tilted and empty. She stared. It didn't take her long to see that the liz-thing wasn't there.

Frantically she scrambled around her room. Maybe Blackberry had only removed the creature. Maybe kittens didn't like the taste of rare, valuable, one-of-a-kind lizard types. She searched in every nook and cranny. If the liz-thing was under the radiator or bed, she would see it. After all, hadn't she found it beneath Foster's refrigerator?

But all her searching was in vain. There was no liz-thing, not even a part of it, anywhere in her room. Her heart sank. Stumbling to her feet, she regarded the black ball of fur curled against her pillow. Blackberry was deeply asleep, the way she had seen him so often at Flint Farm after a long, hard playtime and a big, nourishing meal.

16 *It wasn't until* the middle of the afternoon that Ben made his breakthrough. From the moment lunch was over and Daisy had been taken to her room for a nap, he worked hard at the computer. He would have liked some help, but his parents were taking advantage of Daisy's downtime to get some of their own things done.

At least Ben had peace and quiet. He knew it wouldn't last.

The breakthrough appeared first as a picture and then, when

he was able to sort things out, as information that began to tie in with what he had already learned.

But he had to reconsider the liz-thing's identity. The animal pictured on the screen forced him to. It wasn't a lizard or a dinosaur embryo, but a fossil amphibian found in a fossilized tree stump where, more than three hundred million years ago, it had become trapped and died. The amphibian looked so much like the liz-thing that he couldn't keep from shouting, "Bingo!"

"Ssh," warned his mother from the living room. "Daisy's sleeping."

Ben nodded. No one wanted Daisy to stay asleep more than he did.

The more he read what came up on the screen, the more excited he became. This little animal had lived during the late Carboniferous period when reptiles began to evolve from amphibians. That had been at the beginning of the age of dinosaurs. So the liz-thing might still be a link with dinosaurs. A living link could be even older and rarer and more valuable than a dinosaur embryo.

He jumped up and ran to telephone Kate and Foster.

"We need a meeting," he told Kate.

"I might not be able to," she said. "I'm very busy with my kitten." This wasn't exactly true. She was busy watching Blackberry in the hope that he might eventually lead her to the remains of the liz-thing and possibly even to the whole animal hiding away somewhere. But since Blackberry had scarcely budged in the last two hours, Kate wasn't doing very much of anything.

"Can't you just leave it for a while?" Ben asked.

"No," Kate told him. "Blackberry might need me when he wakes up."

Ben thought a minute. "Okay. We'll meet in your room. I'll call Foster."

"No!" Kate shouted into the phone. "Not in my room. Too many people might upset Blackberry."

"Listen, Kate, this is really big. We have to get together."

Kate clutched the phone so hard her knuckles turned white. How long could she keep Ben from learning that at this very moment there was no liz-thing? She needed more time. If Blackberry hadn't actually eaten it, it might still turn up. "Call Foster," she said, stalling. "Then call me back after you guys decide where and when."

Ben took this to be a reluctant agreement to meet with them after all. "Great!" he told her. "You won't believe what I found out."

Kate didn't respond to this statement. All she could think of was what he hadn't yet found out.

Foster told Ben he was going to the library with his father. He didn't mention that he was looking for dragons. "I'll call you when I get back," he said.

"No," said Ben, "let's decide on a time and place now."

"Okay," Foster agreed without much enthusiasm.

"Kate's house," Ben said quickly. "Five o'clock."

"Okay," Foster answered. He hung up without saying good-bye. Ben could tell that in Foster's mind he was already some-place else.

Back on the phone with Kate, Ben told her about the meeting and its importance.

"I might not be able to," Kate said again.

"You have to," Ben insisted.

"I might be working for Miss Ladd," she told him.

"I thought you had to stay with the kitten."

"I did. I do." Kate didn't know what to say next. "But you know Miss Ladd counts on me to help with her outdoor stuff."

Ben nodded. "So do it before. Or after."

"I'll see," Kate said. "I'm not sure yet."

Ben sighed. Then he informed her that it made all the sense in the world to meet in her room since they needed another good hard look at the liz-thing.

He felt almost mean holding back, not letting her in on his discovery that after all it wasn't a dinosaur embryo or even a lizard. But she would learn all this before long. That is, she would learn it if she managed to get away from Miss Ladd when he and Foster came over to meet in her room.

17 After one last glance around her room, Kate swept up Blackberry and carried him downstairs.

"Where are you going?" her dad asked. "I thought we agreed the kitten would stay inside for the first week or so."

"I'm not letting him go free," Kate said. "I'm just showing him to Miss Ladd."

"Oh." Dad nodded.

"If Ben and Foster show up, tell them—" But if Dad told them anything, it would be the truth or what he believed to be the truth.

"I'll tell them where you are," he said helpfully.

Clutching Blackberry so hard that he began to squirm, Kate dashed outside and across the yard to Miss Ladd's driveway. She had to wait so long for Miss Ladd to let her in that she was afraid Ben would catch her there. Not working. Not doing anything to keep her from his important meeting. But finally the front door opened and Miss Ladd welcomed Kate in.

Almost at once Kate realized that this parlor was no place for Blackberry to run loose, even for a few minutes. Everywhere she looked there were breakable vases and small porcelain figures and lamps with tassels inviting kitten play.

"You don't look as happy as I would have expected to see you today," Miss Ladd said.

Kate nodded and gulped. All at once an awful sense of loss came flooding over her. Not the loss of the liz-thing, but of her love for the kitten. She had been so worried about what Ben would say and do that she hadn't been aware of how her own feelings could be changed. Blinking back tears, she blurted, "Blackberry ate the lizard!"

"What lizard?" Miss Ladd asked.

"Ben's."

"Ben has a lizard?" Miss Ladd exclaimed.

Kate nodded. "He found it. We had it in Foster's bowl in my room because Daisy fiddles with everything."

Looking slightly puzzled, Miss Ladd considered Blackberry. Then she shook her head. "Your kitten doesn't seem big enough or hungry enough to eat a lizard. How big is it?"

Without letting Blackberry go, Kate tried to show with her fingers.

"Well," said Miss Ladd encouragingly, "if it was a baby,

maybe there are more at the shop where it came from. I don't think we have any native lizards."

"Ben found it right here in the ditch on Flint Farm Road. He thinks it might be an embryo, only he's not sure. It's like some dinosaur embryo he saw in a magazine."

Miss Ladd smiled and frowned almost at the same time. Then she picked up the telephone, dialed, and waited. "Frank," she said finally, "do you know whether anyone has released a baby lizard into the wild?" She listened a moment, and then she tried to explain what she knew about Ben's lizard. "What?" she asked. "Wait for what?"

She pulled the phone away from her head. Then she spoke into it again. "Frank?" Then she hung up. Turning to Kate, she said, "That was strange. Frank told me to wait a minute, and now he doesn't seem to be there."

Kate thought there wasn't anything strange about Mr. Torpor being strange, but she didn't say so. It was nearly time for Ben and Foster to arrive. Even though it was too soon for garden work, maybe there was something she could be doing outside for Miss Ladd. That would make part of what she had told Ben true, and it would also keep her too busy for the meeting.

A knock on the door sent her into a panic. Was Ben coming for her already? She stepped aside as Miss Ladd opened the door wide. There stood Mr. Torpor, his shoulders slightly stooped to keep his head from hitting the top of the doorframe. He was holding a large roll of paper.

"Frank," Miss Ladd said to him, "you told me to wait."

"Yes," he answered, "and here I am." He unrolled the sheet

of paper to show her a painting of creatures walking or swimming or lying in a circle. "Does this help?"

Miss Ladd examined the picture. "How can it help? Oh, I see, the lizard."

"Actually Foster calls that one a dragon," Mr. Torpor told her. "It's on its way to becoming the dinosaur. Or maybe it's the other way around."

"Interesting," murmured Miss Ladd. Then she turned to Kate. "Does this one look like your lizard?"

Kate peered down at the painting, which was spread out over the sofa. Clutching the kitten with one hand, she pointed. "That one there," she declared.

"What, the salamander?" Miss Ladd exclaimed. "I thought Ben's was a lizard."

"We're not sure what it is exactly," Kate said, thinking that the only thing she knew for certain was that it had become Blackberry's lunch.

"Ben found it in the ditch," Miss Ladd said to Mr. Torpor.

"An early trekker," he responded. "Not warm enough. They seldom make it."

Kate said, "Ben saved it. It was fine."

"It could be the first," Mr. Torpor declared.

The first? So Ben was right. The liz-thing really was rare and special and valuable and one of a kind! And eaten!

Mr. Torpor and Miss Ladd were both speaking at once. They sounded like conspirators. Mystified, Kate could make no sense of what they were saying.

18 *Foster lugged his* dragon books to the liz-thing meeting only to find that Kate wasn't there. Her father directed him to Miss Ladd's, where Kate let him in. That was a relief. He never knew what to say to Miss Ladd.

He needn't have worried. Miss Ladd was in the middle of some kind of meeting with Mr. Torpor. It sounded as though the meeting were about the weather.

Then he noticed his own painting. "What's this doing here?" he asked Kate.

"Mr. Torpor brought it," she told him. "Because of the liz-thing. Only now they're talking about when it's going to rain."

Foster tried to show Mr. Torpor the books he had borrowed from the library. But Mr. Torpor just nodded vaguely and went on talking to Miss Ladd.

Foster turned to Kate. "What's rain got to do with the liz-thing?"

"I don't know. They started off talking about the lizard. Which it isn't," she added.

"Not a lizard?" Foster asked.

"Not really," she answered. "Listen, Foster, could you find Ben and tell him . . . tell him . . ."

"Tell him to come here?"

"No!" Kate cried, startling Blackberry.

Miss Ladd and Mr. Torpor paused to glance at her.

Kate's voice dropped. "Just tell him this isn't a good time."

"Why isn't it?" Foster asked. He didn't feel like delivering any message to Ben. If only Mr. Torpor would talk to him. Foster had counted on the books' just naturally leading to more painting. Home was the wrong place to try out a new dragon circle. Foster's father and Adele seemed almost as upset when they found sketches of dragons lying around as they had been when all the drawings and paintings were shapes.

Kate beckoned Foster toward the window. She whispered, "Something happened to the liz-thing, or whatever it is now. I can't find it. So I don't want Ben in my room yet."

"You want me to help look for it?"

"I don't know," she told him. How could she allow him to look when she knew it was gone?

Miss Ladd, who couldn't miss hearing her, said, "I'm sure you can find another one. Don't you think so, Frank?"

"Very likely," Mr. Torpor responded.

"There's more?" Kate exclaimed. "Where? How do you know? Are you sure?"

Mr. Torpor took his time answering. "The ditch, maybe. In a hollow stump. Under blowdowns. Some get trapped in window wells."

Kate dashed to the door.

"Not yet," Miss Ladd told her. "After dark."

Kate's heart sank. "I'm not allowed out then."

"Maybe Frank will take you," Miss Ladd suggested. "He usually looks for salamanders this time of year. Makes sure a few early ones reach their destination."

Mr. Torpor cast a glance Miss Ladd's way and then sighed.

Foster hugged the books to his chest. "Can I come, too?" he asked.

Kate looked from one adult to the other. Quiet, gentle Miss

Ladd was being bossy; tall, bent Mr. Torpor was giving in with a slow, silent nod.

"Can we keep it secret?" Kate asked.

"Not from parents," Miss Ladd told her. "As for Ben, you have to decide for yourself whether you want to leave him out."

"Only for a little while," Kate said. "Only until we get another liz—" She broke off under Miss Ladd's steady gaze.

"Salamander," Miss Ladd corrected. "You want to catch another spotted salamander. And then what? Fool Ben into thinking it's the one he found?"

Why not? thought Kate. What harm could it do? "If Ben can't tell the difference . . ." she started to say. Then she faltered, mumbling, "I don't know."

Foster said, "It was Ben's idea to keep it in your room. He can't blame you if it got away."

Kate could feel Miss Ladd's eyes on her. She whispered, "Maybe Blackberry ate it."

"No way," said Foster. "This little kitten?"

Kate nodded. "The liz-thing wasn't very big."

"Ben thinks it's an embryo dinosaur," Foster said to Mr. Torpor. "That's what got me thinking about dragons and how they had to start out little, too, even the giant ones. After a while that's what our liz-thing seemed like—a baby dragon."

Mr. Torpor nodded. "Perfectly reasonable. I'm sure you're not the first person to connect reptiles and amphibians with dragons. But spotted salamanders are not at all dragonlike. And these days fewer than ever make it to the breeding pools."

"You mean they're endangered?" Kate asked.

"Well, yes, that, too," Mr. Torpor replied. "Primarily

because of acid rain. They need rain, you see. Their bodies require moisture when they emerge from the ground. The rain protects them on their way to the ponds where they breed, but it tends to be most acid right now before the trees leaf out. Leaves help to neutralize acidity."

Miss Ladd said, "Frank, you're lecturing. Cut the long words. Show them."

Mr. Torpor nodded gloomily. "All right," he said. But he couldn't keep from adding, "Still, the immediate danger is traffic. You'll see that before long. First there's just a trickle of the little creatures. I expect we'll find some of those this evening. A lot of them die before they can make it to water. But most of the salamanders stay put until conditions are just right. Then, when the night temperature rises and the rain falls, they move up and out. With most of the population migrating at once, many are killed."

"How come I've never seen them?" Foster asked. "How come Ben's was the first?"

"They shy away from light," Mr. Torpor told him. "After living underground all winter, they migrate in the dark. And since most of their breeding pools hold water only in the spring and early summer, the young must develop into land dwellers before their ponds dry up, or else they dry up, too."

"It sounds awful," Kate said with a shudder. "It sounds impossible."

"It's not impossible," Miss Ladd remarked, "but I agree it seems inconvenient."

"But that's what an amphibian is," Mr. Torpor declared. "At one stage it lives in water, at a later stage on land or underground. To complete the life cycle, it returns to the pool or pond where it hatched."

"That's good," Kate exclaimed. "It probably misses swimming. If it has to spend all winter nearly dry, at least it gets to go back to its best place."

Mr. Torpor said, "But—"

"Frank!" Miss Ladd raised a warning hand. "Just show them what they need to see," she told him.

Once again Mr. Torpor bowed to her command.

19

Waiting outside for Kate and Foster, Ben could barely contain himself. He wasn't sure how they would react to his news. He didn't want them to lose interest when they learned that the liz-thing wasn't a dinosaur embryo after all. He would have to impress them with its importance as an amphibian that was just like the kind that lived hundreds of millions of years ago.

But he'd better not overdo it. If he convinced them that it was a really big deal, they could insist on their share of the credit. Kate would be the hardest to handle. She would probably remind him that she had provided safekeeping for the liz-thing. What else? Well, there had been that meal moth. Kate could be tough. Still, she was all wrapped up in her kitten. Would she care if he took back his rare, valuable, first-of-its-kind amphibian?

It was harder to imagine what might go on inside Foster's

head. Would he feel cheated if Ben, and Ben alone, faced the television cameras? Probably not. Foster wasn't the sort of kid who could handle being in the spotlight. Anyway, Ben would make sure that Kate and Foster were included. He would thank them publicly just the way people getting awards thanked their wives and husbands and producers. Ben had seen how it was done.

He didn't expect to see Mr. Torpor come along behind Kate and Foster. If Mr. Torpor stayed with them, Ben would have to postpone the meeting. So far the only grown-ups who knew about the creature's existence were his parents and Kate's, and he was pretty sure that none of them had a clue to what it really was. The longer things stayed that way, the better. Not that Mr. Torpor seemed like the kind of person who would take over from kids. Even when he tramped, slow motion, across the fields and through the woods, he kept to himself. Still, you never knew.

"Hi," said Kate. The kitten draped in her arms was sound asleep.

"Hi," Ben said to her.

Foster didn't speak. He just stood there with his books.

Mr. Torpor held up a roll of paper and said to Foster, "Want me to take this back?"

Foster nodded.

"Want me to take the books, too?"

Foster shook his head. Since he wouldn't be painting tonight after all, he wanted them in his room when he went to bed.

It seemed to Ben that something strange was going on. Did the others suspect what he was about to reveal? But there was

58

no way they could have gotten wind of his discovery. "We need a game plan," he said.

Mr. Torpor said, "See you later then," and walked past them to the road.

Kate said, "We have one. Sort of. Because it's not a lizard." She plunged on. "It might not be— It isn't—" She glanced at Foster. He wasn't about to help out. She looked back toward Miss Ladd's house. She supposed Miss Ladd was standing at her window. Keeping watch? Miss Ladd expected Kate to be truthful.

"I already know," Ben told her. "We must've come across the same information."

Kate faltered. Even if she had no idea what Ben was talking about, she'd better carry on as though she understood. "We'll get some tonight, though," she added. "A few usually start out ahead of all the rest. Like the one you found."

Ben scowled. This wasn't going right. "The rest? There's more?"

Kate nodded vigorously. "Aren't there, Foster?"

Foster said, "The males go first. The females follow. They usually wait for rain. Mr. Torpor says it's supposed to rain tomorrow night. It'll be their time to migrate."

Ben couldn't figure out what rain had to do with his discovery. He didn't like the idea of lots of rare, valuable creatures within everyone's grasp. "Does Mr. Torpor know about it?" he asked. "Who told him? It was supposed to stay secret."

Kate shifted uncomfortably. She said, "Let me put Blackberry down. I mean, up. Upstairs in my room. I'll be right back." She dashed into the house and up to her room. Blackberry purred as she settled him against her pillow. Without even glancing at the bowl on her bureau, she ran downstairs.

"Almost suppertime," her father called from the kitchen.

"We have to go out afterward," she shouted back. "With Mr. Torpor. It's special."

Her mother spoke up. "What about?"

"Nature," she yelled as she slammed the door behind her.

Ben was saying, "I don't get it." His face had gone red.

Foster shrugged. "I know. Just when you think everything fits, it falls apart. I was into dragons. Dragons are a lot more interesting than salamanders."

Ben said, "But the one on the computer was like predinosaur. That's before even reptiles." How could the creature Ben had found in the ditch turn out to be ordinary? How could all his hard work lead to nothing? His scenario with television cameras and news reporters began to dissolve like a movie fadeout. "I don't believe it," he declared. "Mr. Torpor doesn't know everything. Maybe he's on to something else. I bet he hasn't even seen a picture of the fossil amphibian that was trapped in a tree stump millions of years ago."

"Tree stumps!" Kate exclaimed, finally daring to speak out. "That's just where we're supposed to look for one. In a ditch or a hollow log or stump. It's suppertime," she added quickly. "You guys stop by for me later, okay?" She didn't wait for a reply. Things were moving along so fast now it seemed possible that by the time she broke the news to Ben about his liz-thing and Blackberry, she might have another salamander to take its place.

20 *Ben had trouble* taking in most of what Foster had told him. All he really understood was that fame had slipped from his grasp. At first he saw Mr. Torpor as the spoiler. But it didn't take long before Ben placed the blame squarely on Foster and Kate. Not that they had actually stolen his glory. But they had given away his secret and teamed up with an adult. The way Ben saw it, they had canceled their claim to the liz-thing.

"Me go, too," Daisy insisted, whacking her spoon on the table.

"You're too little," Ben told her. "You wouldn't like it. It'll be dark."

For once Ben's father agreed. Ben had been working hard on his science project. This time he would not have his sister tagging along after him.

Ben heaved a sigh. Now all he had to do was shake off the others. He figured that would be no problem with slow Mr. Torpor. But what about Kate and Foster?

It wasn't totally dark when Foster came by for him. Walking along, the boys had to step back from the pavement as cars zoomed past at highway speed. Even on the weekend, drivers using the road for a shortcut seemed in a terrific hurry to get to town.

With flashlights on, the boys crossed over to Kate's house. She was ready.

"What's the knapsack for?" Ben asked her, wishing he'd brought one, too.

Kate shrugged. "Just in case." She wasn't about to admit that she had a mayonnaise jar in it.

She was determined to stash away a salamander to put in the glass mixing bowl on her bureau. She was counting on the darkness to help her pull this off. As soon as she had one good liz-thing replacement, she would work along with the others and be a good team player again. Afterward.

Mr. Torpor was equipped with a pail and a powerful flashlight in hand. He inspected the children. Boots, yes. Jackets, good. Flashlights, well, not quite . . . Foster's was feeble. It was the one they had used when they were looking for the liz-thing under the refrigerator.

Mr. Torpor pulled something from his pocket and placed it on Foster's head. It was a kind of hat harness with a headlamp in front and a battery behind. Ben's heart surged with envy. Quickly he offered his flashlight to Foster. But Foster said he was fine this way. The headlight left both his hands free. He marched off behind Mr. Torpor, his light showing the way to Ben and Kate, who followed.

Mr. Torpor was speaking to Foster. It was so unfair, thought Ben, who couldn't hear. Why bother to try? The only thing he needed to know was that Foster had turned his back on the team to go along with Mr. Torpor like some grown-up.

But after they had crossed the road and tramped into the woods, it occurred to Ben that it might serve his purposes for Foster to keep Mr. Torpor company. If only Ben knew his way around here better. Maybe he ought to pay some attention to what Mr. Torpor was saying after all.

"Pools that fill up in early spring with meltwater and dry out later on are called vernal pools," Mr. Torpor explained in his low, flat voice. "Spotted salamanders return to the same pools each year to breed. The young remain in the pool until they become lung-breathing adults without gills. If the water becomes polluted or the ponds dry up too soon, the next generation is wiped out."

Was Mr. Torpor taking them to a pond to fish salamanders out of the water? Ben didn't ask. He wanted Mr. Torpor to get used to not hearing from him. That way, if he slipped off on his own awhile, Mr. Torpor wouldn't notice.

Ben still hadn't figured out where to slip to and what to look for. He hadn't been looking for anything that day he set eyes on his amphibian. It had just been there, and in broad daylight. So maybe something else would turn up, something no one else would notice, something different and special like his dinosaur embryo. That would have been so cool.

Hanging back, Ben played his flashlight around without seeing much of anything. A hooting brought him to a standstill. How far afield should he go by himself?

"Great horned owl," Mr. Torpor was telling Foster. "The notes tumble down the scale like that."

"Is the owl hunting?" Foster asked.

"When they hunt, they're silent," Mr. Torpor told him. "Like cats," he added.

Thinking of Blackberry, Kate shivered.

Mr. Torpor turned aside and crouched in front of a rotten log. Foster leaned over, lighting the area with the headlamp. Kate and Ben watched as Mr. Torpor peeled away a layer of moss and groped beneath the log. After a moment he replaced the moss. Then his long fingers probed inside the log. With-drawing his hand, he beamed his light inside, shook his head, and rose creakingly to his feet.

On they went, stopping whenever Mr. Torpor came to a likely place.

They were nearing the pond when Mr. Torpor came upon the first salamander of the evening. Everyone, even Ben, crowded close to get a good look at it.

Too much like his rare, valuable, first-of-its-kind amphibian, Ben decided. Unless he came up with something entirely new, maybe a superspecimen, he was finished.

A perfect match, thought Kate, wishing she had found it by herself and had already stashed it safely in the mayonnaise jar.

Full of life, Foster realized. Livelier than the one that had spent the night under the refrigerator. This one didn't want to be caught.

Now Mr. Torpor went down on his hands and knees to burrow in the crevice of a lichen-coated rock. He and Foster had their heads together when Ben clambered up a slope to reach another tree trunk. Beaming his flashlight back and forth, he saw nothing that looked alive, nothing worth his notice.

Meanwhile Kate dropped back and lowered herself beside a tree stump. Peering inside, she saw only leaves and moss. But at the base of the stump her hand brushed something wet. She gasped. Here was a salamander, trapped in the beam of her flashlight. She shrugged off the knapsack, reached for the jar, and unscrewed the lid. Then she brought the jar down over the salamander, slid her hand beneath it, turned it up,

and dropped wet leaves and moss and dirt and one liz-thing replacement in the jar, which she covered and returned to her knapsack.

She looked toward the other lights. No one had seen the capture. Now Ben would never have to know what Blackberry had done. Of course she could still change her mind. But if she decided to tell him later on, at least she would be able to choose her time.

She began to hunt in earnest for more salamanders to add to the few that scrambled around in the bottom of Mr. Torpor's pail.

Ben hunted in vain. All his luck seemed to have run out at once. When he saw Kate stoop and gather an amphibian in her hands and take it to the pail, he didn't even resent it anymore. He just felt dismal and let-down. A loser, that's what he was.

Mr. Torpor said it was time to take the salamanders to the pond they had been heading for. Probably many more were stirring from their winter sleep, moving closer to the surface of the ground, biding their time, waiting for just the right thaw and rain to keep them moist on their journey.

Foster gazed inside the pail at the tangle of salamanders. Mr. Torpor had been right. There was nothing dragonlike about the lithe, spotted bodies with clawing feet and sleek, waving heads. Creatures of earth and darkness that had burrowed deep beneath the ground all winter, they didn't seem to realize they were trapped as they clambered over one another, struggling to regain their path.

At the edge of the pool Mr. Torpor knelt on the muddy bank. He tilted the pail to let a little water in. Not until all the salamanders were swimming vigorously inside the pail did he lower it below the surface to set them free.

21 *Leading the way* back to the road, Mr. Torpor began to describe some of the devices he had invented over the years to save the salamanders from being run over. Mostly it was a losing battle. There was a limit to what one person could do.

That ditch had been last year's effort. It was designed to slow the migration just before the creatures started across the road. Then, before they climbed up and out, he would scoop them into his pail and deposit them on the other side. He had hoped to dig all along the road where the salamanders crossed, but some commuter had complained to the town about the roadside hazard, and the highway department had made him stop. It always seemed to end up like that.

Even Ben, steeped in his own dejection, was impressed. "That's a lot of digging," he exclaimed. "How long would it have taken?"

Mr. Torpor couldn't tell. He had just gone to work on it, all by himself, where year after year he had seen so many salamanders run over. "They were here before us," Mr. Torpor said. "It's their path we've invaded with our road and our cars."

Recalling what he had learned so far about amphibians' being the earliest connection between fish and reptiles, like lizards, Ben couldn't keep from chiming in. "Maybe spotted salamanders were here before dinosaurs."

"Maybe," Mr. Torpor agreed. "Anyway, it's their right-of-way."

"You can't train them to go somewhere else?" asked Kate.

There was a smile in Mr. Torpor's voice as he replied, "I suspect it would take millions of years for them to unlearn one route, let alone adopt another. I don't think any of us has that much time. And it's hard to buck what we call progress."

"Except," Ben blurted, "if we all try. Not just one person."

"Possibly," Mr. Torpor responded. "I heard of a community that dug a tunnel under a road to allow spotted salamanders to get to their breeding pool. Of course that took advance planning. If tomorrow night's temperature rises into the forties and we get the rain that's forecast, it's a good bet for the mass migration. That gives us less than twenty-four hours to prepare. And the highway department isn't kindly disposed toward me and my campaign. They think I'm . . ." His voice trailed away.

"What about a roadblock?" Ben asked, warming to the idea as he spoke. They could set up barriers and flares like police trying to catch a getaway car. He would become the defender of spotted salamanders, lowly creatures but deserving of their special niche in the ecosystem. He pictured himself waving and swaggering up to irate drivers. In firm, commanding tones he would explain why they must turn back.

"Why not?" Kate exclaimed. "We have all day tomorrow to get ready. If everyone on Flint Farm Road helps, we can stop the cars."

Mr. Torpor said, "Do you really think so? It takes organization, an all-out effort."

"We can do it!" Ben said. He was back on track again, leading the way. "Cooperation is what we're good at. Right?" He looked to Kate and Foster for confirmation.

Not quite, thought Kate. Lately the three of them had been more like the salamanders in Mr. Torpor's pail, climbing over one another to get nowhere. But she nodded in agreement because of the chance to turn things around.

Back on the road now, they were able to walk four abreast as long as no headlights warned of an oncoming car. Every time one approached, Mr. Torpor shepherded the kids to the side. It was after an especially noisy truck silenced them that Foster finally spoke.

"So we get everyone to help?" he asked. "Every single person on Flint Farm Road?"

"Right," Ben declared. "Starting first thing tomorrow."

"What if it doesn't rain?" Foster continued. "What if we get everyone out on the road and the salamanders don't come?"

"Then we'll call it a practice run," Ben promptly responded.

They all began to speak at once. Now that the rescue plan was launched, more questions cropped up, more suggestions.

All the same, Kate couldn't wait to take her captured specimen home. Even though replacing the eaten liz-thing seemed less urgent now that Ben was set on saving the entire local population of spotted salamanders, she needed to finish what she had begun. Already she felt better just knowing that Blackberry's crime had somehow lost its bite.

22 Ben *suspected that* it might take all day just to fire up the grown-ups. It wasn't easy impressing on them how important the timing was.

"It's a fine idea," his mother told him, "except the after-dark part. Can't you do it earlier?"

He figured the Josephsons across the road were less likely to worry about the nighttime hazards since their kids were already grown and gone.

But Mr. Josephson said, "Only the police can turn back cars from a public road. Residents don't have a legal right to stop traffic."

"What if there's a—a—like an accident or something on the road?"

"Oh." Mr. Josephson thought a moment. "I suppose if there was an obstruction, a danger, that would make a difference."

"Cool!" Ben exclaimed. "So we'll need extra flashlights. And everyone has to wear something white. Okay?" He was on his way before Mr. Josephson could object.

Progress was slow for Kate, too. When her mother had a good look at the spotted salamander coming through the house in the mayonnaise jar, she objected. Apparently she had never actually laid eyes on the first liz-thing. "I thought once you got a kitten of your own you wouldn't need . . . other animals. If that's what this slimy thing is," she added. "Why can't you just be content with Blackberry?"

"I don't want a spotted salamander for a pet," Kate

explained. "They just need to get to their breeding pool. I mean, I'm only keeping this one for a little while."

Her brothers came to her rescue. Stopping traffic had an instant appeal for them, just as it had for Ben. As soon as they vowed to stand in the front lines and flag down drivers, Kate's dad gave in and agreed to help, too.

Encouraged, Kate went on to tackle Mr. and Mrs. Flint. Since they farmed on both sides of the road and resented the way speeding cars interfered with their coming and going, Kate didn't have to say much to convince them to join in the effort.

"This is getting to be a spring event," Mrs. Flint remarked. "Wasn't it around this time last year that you alerted the neighborhood about the sweet corn? It must be the longer, warmer days that bring you all out again. Like the salamanders." She promised to help on the road, and Mr. Flint said he would supply orange cones to set up at each end.

Miss Ladd was already on Mr. Torpor's side, so she was even easier. Rummaging through her costume fabric, she sorted out the right material to make into banners to wave at oncoming cars.

Compared with Ben's and Kate's families, Foster's was a breeze. His father and Adele were so thrilled that he was concerned about real live creatures instead of imaginary ones and they were so pleased that he was involved in a neighborhood cause, they went all out with support. Even though their printshop was normally closed on Sundays, they decided to go in to make posters for the roadblock.

"You want to paint a sample one for us to use?" Dad asked

Foster. "You can do that, can't you? Not a dragon, son, a salamander."

Foster nodded. Of course he could. Why was his father making such a big deal about it?

"Wonderful!" Adele exclaimed. "That's just wonderful!"

Foster, who was really getting somewhere with his dragon drawings, figured he would be back to them as soon as the salamanders were taken care of. Only why, he wondered as he outlined a salamander from memory, why didn't anyone think his dragons were wonderful, too?

23 *All through the* day everyone kept glancing skyward at the low ceiling of cloud from which not one drop of rain fell.

"That's all right," Miss Ladd told Kate. "The longer the rain holds off, the better the chance that when it comes, it will last for the salamanders. They need that wetness for their long trek."

"It can't be all that long," Kate said. "Mr. Torpor says the pond is just down in the woods."

Miss Ladd shook out a remnant of gold cloth. "For the size of them, though," she continued as she flattened the fabric, "for the length of their legs, don't you suppose that's a daunting journey to complete before daybreak?"

Kate recalled the liz-thing scurrying under the refrigerator. But of course that had been like a sprint. She wondered how salamander distance translated into people terms. Maybe their journey to the breeding pool was like the pioneers traveling across the country to settle in the West. But how many people had actually walked? And how long did it take?

"I can't find any Day-Glo," Miss Ladd declared, "but this should show up well, especially in front of headlights." She held up a length of hot pink material. "I can get four banners out of this and highlight them with the gold. We can use gardening stakes. You remember where we put them last fall?"

The first stakes Kate brought indoors were too thin. Miss Ladd sent her back to the shed to look for sturdier, longer ones. By the time Kate found them, Miss Ladd was already working at her sewing machine. She let Kate use the pinking shears to cut gold cloth outlined in the shape of stop signs.

Kate watched Miss Ladd stitch the first stop-sign patch onto the hot pink material.

Miss Ladd glanced up at Kate and remarked, "I thought I might write 'SALAMANDER CROSSING' on it, but that takes up too much space. Besides, all drivers recognize a stop sign."

It was a miracle to Kate the way a bit of fabric could be transformed into an elegant banner to be used just once in the rain. If ever Kate made something so beautiful, she doubted she would be able to let it be ruined so soon. "If you wrote 'CREATURE CROSSING,' it would be ready later on in case some other kinds of animals needed to be helped across the road. Then everyone would be careful of it."

"Good idea," Miss Ladd responded. "Next time we'll plan together."

That made Kate think about the emblem Foster was designing for the poster. After leaving Miss Ladd to her sewing, Kate went home to play with Blackberry until he was ready to nap, and then she set off to find Foster. His room was littered with sketches and drawings of spotted salamanders.

"Did you finish?" she asked. "Which one did you choose?"

Foster, who had been reading on his unmade bed, showed her a picture of a salamander partly curled into the shape of a question mark.

Kate frowned. "This is the one they're using?"

"One like it," he said.

"I don't get the question part," she finally told him.

"There's going to be words underneath." Foster let the paper drift down onto the others. "Dad's doing the words. He says the poster shouldn't be too cluttered. So all it'll say is: 'WILL I SURVIVE?' "

Kate studied the salamander question mark. "It's pretty good," she told him.

Foster shrugged. He almost didn't show her the other drawings. But he needed someone to see his dragons, someone he could count on not to disapprove. So he reached under his bed and swept out a loosely stacked set of pictures. "What about these?" he asked Kate.

Kate gazed at an array of dragonlike creatures, some in flight, some slithering on the ground. "This," she said, pointing to one that had the blunt head of a salamander, "must be the liz-thing's first cousin."

Foster nodded. Kate's recognizing the connection was better than any praise she could have given.

"You should've designed Miss Ladd's banners," she told him. "Except that they'll be rained on. What'll happen to the posters?"

"Plastic," he said. "They'll be like shrink-wrapped. My father and Adele think . . . I don't know what they think, but they don't like me drawing dragons or shapes."

Kate told him he did dragons better than anything else.

"Better than kittens?"

She nodded. "What difference does it make what you draw?"

"I think it's supposed to be real," he answered. "It's healthier or something."

Kate scowled. Dragons were unhealthy? "What about shapes then?" she asked him. "Miss Ladd's doing shapes for the banners."

"She is?" Foster couldn't quite believe that someone as proper as Miss Ladd would make something that people like his father and Adele frowned on.

"Come on back to Miss Ladd's with me," Kate suggested. "Maybe she'll let you make a banner, too, one that's whatever you want it to be."

Foster didn't leap at the idea. He had decided he'd better keep his dragons private from now on, except for the one or two people he could trust. But Kate insisted. If he designed a banner, she would help him cut out the pieces for it. She would carry it, too, so that no one could blame him if anyone thought it was wrong.

At last he gave in. He was sort of curious about what Miss Ladd was up to. A short visit couldn't hurt, especially if Kate was there to do the talking.

24 *Ben was beginning* to think that no one remembered that this had been his idea in the first place. Not only had he found this year's first amphibian, but he had come up with the rescue plan. So how come everyone was busy but him?

He knew he ought to get his mind on something else, but he couldn't just turn himself off. If only there were something for him to do.

He almost went back to Miss Ladd's house, where Foster was drawing on cloth, and Kate, with weird-looking scissors, was cutting out shapes that would become what Foster drew. But their project was too much like arts and crafts, stuff little kids did. Ben was a nuts-and-bolts kind of person. Besides, it was clear that Kate and Foster didn't need him.

He trudged off toward Mr. Torpor's house. The last time Ben had checked in there, Mr. Torpor had invited him to stay and help make armbands with bicycle reflectors for people to wear in the dark. Ben supposed he might as well do that after all. It was better than nothing.

But when he finally found Mr. Torpor behind his house in the shed where he repaired bikes, the armbands were all finished.

Mr. Torpor studied Ben's expression for a moment. "Loose ends?" he asked.

Ben wasn't sure what that meant. He wished Foster were here to interpret. Foster understood Mr. Torpor.

Mr. Torpor stepped outside the shed and tilted his craggy face to the dismal sky. "Ah," he declared, "it's coming."

Ben nodded. Either rain or night. He could only agree.

"We ought to make a record of all this," Mr. Torpor remarked. "Show others what to do. Know cameras?" Mr. Torpor asked him.

Ben nodded. He guessed he knew cameras. But when Mr. Torpor strode into his house, holding the door for Ben, and produced a camera the likes of which Ben had never seen, he shook his head. "Not that kind," he amended.

"It's older," Mr. Torpor informed him. "But it takes fine pictures."

As he began to show Ben how it worked, it gradually dawned on Ben that Mr. Torpor was instructing him. Not only that, but Mr. Torpor was going to entrust Ben with the camera and make him the official rescue photographer.

At first it was kind of scary. What if Ben broke something? But soon he became so fascinated that he stopped worrying. After all, if he could use a computer, he ought to be able to use a machine that had probably been made before computers existed.

"Ideally you'd practice and then see the results," Mr. Torpor told him. "But there's no time for that. So you must simply do your best."

"What happens when it's raining or dark?" Ben asked. "Will the light meter work?"

Mr. Torpor explained and demonstrated and explained some more. Then he had Ben try out the camera with and without the flash attachment. Just when Ben was beginning to enjoy himself, Mr. Torpor sat him down on a kitchen chair and quizzed him on everything he had just been taught. Ben didn't get it all right. But he did begin to learn what questions to ask and even how to figure out some things for himself.

With a final warning about changing film in a dry place and not using too much up until the rescue was under way, Mr. Torpor presented Ben with the camera and an extra roll of film.

Having the safety strap actually placed over his head made Ben feel a little bit like someone receiving an honor. But it was an honor Ben knew he had not yet earned.

25

Figuring to start with a shot of the first amphibian and hoping that Kate had finished at Miss Ladd's, Ben headed back. He was in luck. Kate and Foster were standing outside, showing Kate's family a midnight blue banner with a silver salamander and dragon and lizard in a circle.

"Hold it!" Ben commanded as he raised the camera.

Foster exclaimed, "That's Mr. Torpor's. It's—it's unreplaceable!"

"Irreplaceable," Kate's mother said. "Are you sure you know what you're doing?"

Ben checked the light meter, set the speed, focused, and pressed the trigger.

Even Kate's brothers were impressed "That thing must be an antique," one of them said to Ben. The other one touched the silver dragon and asked, "Where did that come from?"

"Careful," Kate said, snatching the banner away. "We didn't have time to sew the liz-thing circle, so it's just glued for now. It stands for 'Creature Crossing.'"

Foster couldn't say where any dragon came from. All he knew was that it belonged with those other creatures. Maybe they came from one another.

Ben spoke with less than his usual confidence. "I'm allowed to take pictures. I'm supposed to record the rescue." He turned to Kate. "So I thought I'd begin with the first liz-thing."

"Fine," Kate replied, beckoning to him past her family and into the house. She led the way up the stairs and to her closed door. They could hear Blackberry racing around. They could hear something roll across the floor.

Ben said, "Maybe you could hold the liz-thing for me. I want to get a really good picture of it."

"Fine," Kate repeated. With nothing more to worry about, she would agree to anything. Blackberry leaped on her bed and pounced on a toy mouse. Kate walked to her bureau. She removed the sweater that she had draped over the glass bowl and weighted with a book. When she looked down into her homemade terrarium, she could only gasp.

"Where is it?" she cried. She stole a glance at the kitten cavorting on the bed. How could Blackberry have eaten the replacement salamander without dislodging the bowl cover?

Ben, at her side, looked and then reached into the bowl. Digging a bit and probing, he withdrew the salamander. And then he gasped as well. "There's another one!" he said. "Look, Kate, right there."

She peered over and around his hand. "Just a minute," she mumbled, gazing where Ben had loosened the moss and dead leaves. Nearly buried beneath the baby oak a second salamander squirmed and tried to dig itself deeper.

"A second salamander," she said weakly, "or else the first."

She drew a long breath and then blurted, "I put it there. I thought the liz-thing was . . . gone." She couldn't believe it. All this guilt and torment for nothing! If she had dug around the way Ben had in the first place, she might have saved herself all that misery.

Ben had no trouble accepting her explanation. For him it was no big deal. "So let's get a picture of this one and just figure it's the first. Okay?"

She nodded. It was still sinking in that she had panicked for nothing and blamed her kitten. Wrongly? Or had the liz-thing escaped being eaten because it had burrowed out of sight?

"Can we put it on your bed for just a second?" he asked.

"Not yet," she told him, snatching up Blackberry. Then she nodded again. "Okay, go ahead."

Blackberry didn't seem to notice that a spotted salamander had joined the toy mouse in the middle of the bed. Holding the kitten, Kate could feel the rumbling start up in him before she actually heard his purring. Maybe that was because she was able to relax her iron grip at last and cradle him in her arms.

26 *Darkness sifted down* from the sky and overspread the land. But this was still afternoon. Could night fall ahead of its time?

"It's the rain," Mr. Torpor said to the kids, who waited anxiously with him.

Ben stepped forward and aimed the camera at a small procession making its way toward them on the road. Caught between flashlight beams at each end, the shrouded figures seemed to flow together, becoming a single, eerie form. It was almost as if Foster's cutout beasts had dropped from his banner and taken to the road. As soon as the procession halted in front of Mr. Torpor's more powerful light, the fantastic presence dissolved. In its place stood neighbors in raincoats and foul-weather gear.

Assigning positions was confusing because Ben thought he was in charge and Mr. Josephson, who had called the police, thought he was. Kate's brothers said they would quit if they couldn't divert traffic at the highway end of Flint Farm Road. That was where the real action would be. But all the parents united and declared the highway a place for adults. The boys would find plenty of action at the town end, but with less danger from speeding cars.

While Mr. Torpor handed out armbands studded with bike reflectors, Mr. and Mrs. Flint arrived on the scene with a supply of cones, buckets, spatulas, and ladles. Mrs. Flint said that in bygone years she used to scoop up salamanders with a ladle or a spatula to lift them quickly across to the downhill side.

With everyone milling about, no one even looked at the road until one more flashlight beam announced the arrival of someone else. The light weaved and bobbed slowly as it approached. Then Miss Ladd spoke from behind the flashlight, her voice soft but bright. "Seven so far. That I've seen. I've helped one or two that were taking too long."

Everyone stopped moving, as though glued to the spot.

"It's begun," Mr. Torpor declared in an awed whisper.

Then many more flashlights were switched on, and people began to search the road.

"Everyone to their posts," Ben ordered. He figured he

wouldn't have to stick here with the crossing crew. After all, photojournalists had to get around.

Picking their way with care, Mr. and Mrs. Josephson led Kate's brothers off toward the town end of the road. Foster's father and Adele, Kate's father, and Ben's mother all headed for the highway.

"Are the posters in place?" Miss Ladd asked Mr. Torpor.

"Posters and banners and lanterns at each end of the road, and now the orange cones will mark the crossing area."

"I'll go, too," Ben said. "To record what happens."

His mother, who had found a last-minute baby-sitter for Daisy, said, "Don't even think of it. You do all your recording right here."

"This will be a long, wet, chilly vigil," Mrs. Flint told him. "Go easy on the pictures."

For a while the crossing crew was busy finding and moving the oncoming salamanders, which seemed to come in waves. Kate chose to pick them up before they reached the cold, hard road. Ben suggested that everyone keep track of how many they moved so there would be some sort of count to report.

But that turned the rescue into a contest. Mr. Flint pointed out that hurrying could be as rough on the salamanders as cars. These small, soft creatures must be handled gently. So everyone told everyone else to slow down.

Foster was happy. Even though his banner drooped wetly, when unfurled, it proclaimed the dragon connection that had begun for him with the liz-thing. No one, not even his father and Adele, had objected to its emblem. Perhaps they hadn't yet noticed that it showed a circle of beasts, real and imaginary, each leading to and from one another.

Kate was happy, too. Although her aching fingers felt like icicles, she basked in the warmth of renewed love for Blackberry. Because Miss Ladd still maintained that it would always be in his nature to seek prey, every salamander Kate helped across the road became a kind of offering. She supposed that she was shoring up against some future time when Blackberry might prove Miss Ladd right.

Ben was neither happy nor sad. He kept himself too busy to feel much of anything beyond the cold of this rainy night. He had never imagined rescue work could be so boring. Keeping count helped a little. But there had to be more to it. Without understanding why, he knew he must stay poised for action.

So while he worked, he waited for something to happen.

27

Even though everyone was dressed for this weather, the chill struck deep into their bones. Ben's mother and Miss Ladd tried singing to keep themselves warm, but after a time their voices drifted off. When people spoke, it was in a hush. The rain spattered on hoods and hats. The salamanders made no noise at all.

"How many?" Ben demanded. "Foster's up to eleven."

Kate had lost count. "Nine, I think. I have to keep blowing on my fingers."

Ben had only seven. It had been eight until one turned out to be a small stick. But of course he was burdened with the heavy camera under the oversize poncho Mr. Torpor had made him wear to protect it.

"Car!" Mrs. Flint called out.

They formed a barrier across the road and beamed their flashlights at the oncoming vehicle. They all understood the drill. As soon as Mr. Flint gave the word, they were to move to the side of the road. Ben backed off so that he could photograph the scene.

But no one had to scramble for safety after all. The car slowed before it reached the crossing area and pulled over. A man opened its door and stepped onto the road. He had a flashlight, too. "Mind if I join you?" he asked. "Some of the drivers aren't too pleased to be rerouted. I guess they don't realize what salamanders do, I mean, like eating mosquito larvae. Same as bats, these little critters. Right?"

He kept on talking as he walked along. Mr. Flint had to raise a hand and gesture toward the road surface to stop him from stepping on a salamander.

"You're our first car," Ben said to him. "We expected a lot more."

"Well," the man said, "the folks up the road are doing a fine job turning cars away. Good thing it's a Sunday. You won't get your commuter traffic."

Ben took a picture of the man, but after a while his commentary grew tiresome, and Ben set to work to catch up to Foster, who now claimed to have carried seventeen salamanders to the safe side of the road.

"Car!" Mrs. Flint called. The newcomer nearly smeared another salamander in his haste to join the human barrier.

"Another convert?" Miss Ladd wondered out loud.

But this car showed no sign of pulling over or even of slowing.

All at once the grown-ups sounded alarmed. "Over to the side," they ordered. "Get back."

Mr. Flint and Mr. Torpor were the only people allowed to stand in the road. They stood together swinging their flashlights until finally the car had to stop.

A window rolled down. "Out of my way," snarled the driver.

The window on the passenger side rolled down as well. A woman stuck her head out. "Are you people for real?" she demanded. "You've got no right to do this."

"We're only asking drivers to give the salamanders a few hours," Mr. Flint told them quietly. "That's all they need. If you tell us where you're heading, we'll be glad to show you another route."

"None of your business where we're going," the driver retorted. "This is a free country."

Mr. Torpor stooped low to face the driver. "If you insist on going this way, will you go very slowly? Maybe you can stop for any you see and spare them."

"Forget it," the driver told him. "Out of my way."

"Watch it, Frank," Mr. Flint said. "Right there at your foot."

At Mr. Torpor's foot and too close to the car. Mr. Torpor practically had to double over to pick up the salmander. Seeing another dazed by the headlights, he reached for that one, too.

In that same instant the driver gunned the motor. Mr. Torpor lurched and fell to his knees. The car inched toward him, the woman screeching, "Get him out of there."

With all horrified eyes on Mr. Torpor, Ben had no trouble slipping from the roadside ranks. Racing around behind the car, he sidled up until he was close to the front door. He took two pictures in rapid succession, one that would show the front end of the car and Mr. Torpor on the road, the other of the driver, his face contorted with rage. Quick as anything Ben ran back and photographed the license.

As soon as the car shot away, Ben found that his hands were shaking so hard he could barely cover the camera lens. He hoped he had held the camera steady while he was taking the pictures. The police might want that license number.

Everyone surrounded Mr. Torpor, who claimed to be unhurt except for bruised knees and a profound disappointment in some people. For the first time since joining the rescue, the talkative man was at a loss for words.

Mrs. Flint, who was already close to home, went back to her house to make hot chocolate to help people warm up. Miss Ladd and Ben's mother scraped up the few smashed carcasses left in the road. Meanwhile the salamanders kept coming, and the crossing crew kept working.

When the next car approached, creeping at a snail's pace through the crossing area, it helped erase the impression set by the earlier incident.

"After all," Mrs. Flint declared as she dropped two marshmallows into Foster's steaming cup, "we don't even know how many drivers were persuaded to go another way. A couple of bad apples can never really spoil all the good ones."

All of the crossing crew stayed until the rain let up and word came from each end of the road that no cars had tried to turn in during the last twenty minutes. By that time they had all stopped counting salamanders. The vigil had lasted nearly five hours; it was past many bedtimes.

The man who had parked his car and joined the rescuers thanked them as if he had been admitted into an exclusive club. He drove on toward town with great caution.

Everyone else headed home except Mr. Torpor, who decided to keep watch for another hour or so. He took his camera back from Ben just in case something else came up while he was alone. There was nothing, he maintained, as powerful as a loaded camera for keeping people in line.

Back in her room, Kate found the mixing bowl still covered. On her bed Blackberry stretched and yawned. She had to shift him a little to make room for herself. Then she crawled under the covers and snuggled into the warm spot he had left.

Foster propped up his banner with books so that it would be the first thing he saw in the morning. Where do dragons come from? he asked himself sleepily. Are they first things or things yet to be? But he couldn't stay awake long enough to ponder these questions.

After

The next afternoon Ben and Kate and Foster took the salamanders from Kate's room down to the pool in the woods.
Everything was drenched from last night's rain, making them
wet all over again.

They dipped the mixing bowl into the water and watched
Kate's small garden float to the surface. The miniature tree
toppled as the salamanders wriggled past it to swim free. The
pool churned with invisible life, leaves and twigs and twiglike
forms tumbling toward the surface and then dropping from
sight.

The weekly newspaper carried a brief story about the salamander rescue on Flint Farm Road and a full page of pictures
to illustrate it. The photographer's name and age appeared in
very small type. There was a photo of Mrs. Flint wielding her
spatula, one of Kate's brothers beside a poster, one of all
the neighbors lined up across the road, one of Kate with a
salamander in each hand, one of Foster's dragon circle, one
of the helpful stranger talking to Miss Ladd, and two that
recorded the confrontation with the angry people in the car.

Just about everyone else who had joined in the effort was seen in the background of at least one of the pictures—everyone except Ben. He didn't mind, though. He knew where he had been the whole time, and that was all that mattered.